The water began to bubble and boil....

When the water calmed down, I saw a little hand come thrusting through the surface.

"He's drowning!" hissed Sarah. "Go save him, Anthony!"

I started forward, but Albert was already hauling himself onto the edge of the sink. He shook his head, spattering tiny drops of water in all directions. Then he stood, stretched his arms, threw his head back, and growled.

It was a tiny sound, but terrifying nonetheless.

He walked along the edge of the basin, looking puzzled. "What a strange white road," he muttered.

I cleared my throat.

Albert glanced up at me and Sarah. "*Monsters!*" he screamed. Then he dove back into the sink.

Look for these other Bruce Coville titles from Scholastic:

Bruce Coville's Book of Monsters
Bruce Coville's Book of Aliens
Bruce Coville's Book of Ghosts
Bruce Coville's Book of Nightmares
Bruce Coville's Book of Spine Tinglers
Bruce Coville's Book of Magic

and coming soon:

Bruce Coville's Book of Aliens II
(November 1996)
Bruce Coville's Book of Ghosts II
(January 1997)
Bruce Coville's Book of Nightmares II
Bruce Coville's Book of Spine Tinglers II
Bruce Coville's Book of Magic II

BRUCE COVILLE'S
BOOK OF

MONSTERS

MORE TALES TO GIVE YOU THE CREEPS

II

Compiled and edited by
Bruce Coville

Assisted by
Lisa Meltzer

Illustrated by
John Pierard

A GLC Book

AN
APPLE
PAPERBACK

SCHOLASTIC INC.
New York Toronto London Auckland Sydney

To my friends at H.W. Smith Elementary

ISBN 0-590-85292-2

12   11   10   9   8   7   6   5   4   3   2   1   6   7   8   9/9   0   1/0

Printed in the U.S.A.   40

First Scholastic printing, August 1996

CONTENTS

Contents

INTRODUCTION:

WE'RE BA-A-A-ACK!

All right, all right. I give up. You win. Here it is: another book of monsters.

I certainly didn't intend to do this. The original plan when I started this series of anthologies was to do four books, one each for monsters, aliens, ghosts, and nightmares. But you little beasts have gobbled them up so voraciously that here we are on our seventh volume. And there are five more yet to come!

(That's right, this is the first of another full round of Monsters, Aliens, Ghosts, Nightmares, Spine Tinglers, and Magic heading your way. When we're done, we'll have an even dozen of these books. Maybe if I lose what's left of my mind, I'll do one more, to make it a terrifying thirteen.)

The beginning of this round is a good time for me to make something clear: I couldn't do this without a lot of help! Part of that help comes from all the terrific authors who provide stories for these books, of course. But I think it's time for you to meet one of the people who works behind the scenes: the fabulous Lisa Meltzer, the editor at General Licensing Company who helps me put these books together.

Here's how it works. When we know we're going to assemble some new anthologies, we send word to writers we think can create the kind of stories we want. The writers start thinking, and after a while stories start to arrive—more and more of them as the deadline draws near. Some come by regular mail; many reach us by e-mail on the "information superhighway."

Lisa goes through the initial stack and chooses the best, which she sends on to me to read. This is the most exciting part of the process—but also the most frustrating, because we almost always have more good stories than we can possibly use.

What to do? How to choose?

Well, one way we make our selections is by *balance.* We try to have short stories and long stories, funny stories and sad stories, modern stories and stories that take place in other times. The stories only have to have two things in common: They have to be good, and they have to match the theme of the book.

Next the editing starts. Lisa and I discuss

what each story needs to make it better—how it can be clearer, tighter, more scary, or more funny (or both). Then we contact the writers and ask for revisions. Some stories need only a little tinkering, others go through as many as six or seven full drafts before we are satisfied. *All* of them have *some* changes. (Just in case you were wondering.)

At the same time our illustrator, John Pierard, starts making sketches to show us his ideas for the drawings he would like to include. Just like our authors, he often has to make revisions. For example, sometimes John has a *great* idea for a picture, but the drawing will give away a surprise in the story. In those cases I always ask him to think of something else to draw, since I know kids often peek ahead at the pictures.

While all this is going on, Lisa is usually bugging me to get my own story written. (In fact, even as I write this introduction, all the other stories are finished, but my own is not done yet. Bad! Bad Bruce. Bad, bad!)

I do have an excuse, which is that I like to wait until last so that I can do something different to round out the book. (But the truth is, sometimes I just get behind.)

Anyway, like all the other writers, I have to do my story more than once. Don't think Lisa takes it easy on me just because my name is on the cover! I often have to do six or seven drafts myself. And just when I think I've finally got a story perfect, she usually finds some way for me to make it better.

When all the stories are ready, the book goes to a copyeditor, who reads it to check for spelling and grammar and punctuation and facts and inconsistencies (like whether a character has blue eyes on one page and brown eyes on the next).

Then everybody makes a few more corrections.

Then the stories go to the typesetter, who puts them in the very neat format you see in the book.

Then Lisa and the authors and I all read them *again*. This is our last chance to make changes and corrections.

Whew! It makes me tired just thinking about it.

But I'll tell you something. When I finally hold the book in my hands, I forget all the work and the fussing and the fixing and just smile like a monster on the night of a full moon.

Okay, now you know where these books come from. But put that aside for now.

The monsters are getting restless.

"Forget this introduction stuff," they're

snarling. "Turn the page. *We want to claw our way into your brain.*"

Yeah, I know you think you can handle them.

But maybe you'd better leave a light on tonight.

Just in case . . .

Bruce Coville

Sometimes stories start with a title. As a parent and a former teacher, I confess I've used the phrase "little monsters" plenty of times. When I was trying to think of a story for this book, it kept coming to mind.
So I decided to take it literally, and write about . . . little monsters.
(I threw in the monkey and the trip to the haunted house as a bonus.)

LITTLE MONSTERS
(Part 1 of "The Monsters of Morley Manor")

Bruce Coville

I. Bargaining

If my stupidhead little sister hadn't put the monkey in the bathtub we might never have had to help the monsters get big. But she did, so we did, which as it turned out was probably just as well for everyone on the planet, all things considered.

I got the monsters at a garage sale. Actually, it was more like a whole house sale. And not just any house; it was the old Morley place at the end of Willow Street.

Everyone knew Morley Manor. It was the weirdest house in town, so scary we didn't even trick-or-treat there. It had three towers, leaded-glass windows, and a big iron fence with spikes on the top. My father liked to claim it even had its own weather system, since it always seemed darker and gloomier there than anywhere else in town.

When Mr. Morley died (at the age of ninety-seven!) none of his relatives wanted to move into the house. In fact, *no one* wanted to live in the place. The guy who finally bought it planned to tear it down and build a new house altogether.

The weekend before the wreckers were supposed to start, my parents went to a florists' convention, leaving Gramma Walker to take care of me and my sister.

That same weekend Mr. Morley's great-niece had a sale to get rid of all the stuff in the house. Every kid in town went, even though it was pouring rain. After all, it was the last chance we would ever have to get a look inside the old place.

The house had high ceilings, dark woodwork, and doors just as creaky as you would have expected. It must have been beautiful once, but I could see why no one would want to buy it now. It looked as if that weather system my father talked about had existed inside as well as outside. The house was damp and moldy, and peeling wallpaper hung down in long strips, leaving bare spots where dark patches of mildew had started to grow.

I found a lot of things I wanted to buy: weird little statues, candleholders shaped like demons, a chess set with stone pieces that looked as if they had been carved out of someone's nightmare. But they were all too expensive: *way* too expensive, given the fact that I had spent almost all my money on a new batch of game cards just a few days earlier.

Then my little sister found something I thought maybe I *could* afford, though it was hard to tell, since it didn't have a price tag. I was studying a roped-off stairway that had a sign saying ABSOLUTELY NO ONE ADMITTED PAST THIS POINT and wondering what would happen if I *did* go past that point when Sarah grabbed my sleeve and said, "Come *here*, Anthony. You *have* to see this!"

(That's the way she talks; like half her words are in italics.)

I didn't go right away; I don't want her getting the idea I'll do something as soon as she asks me to. But after a minute I followed her to the

3

library. (Yeah, this house was so fancy it had its own library. Only the library smelled pretty bad, because of the mildew and everything.)

"Look!" she said proudly.

Sitting on a small, round table was something that looked like a wooden cigar box. Carved into its top was a strange design of interlocking circles.

"I didn't see that when I was in here before," I said.

"It was hidden behind the encyclopedia," replied Sarah, nodding toward one of the shelves. "This old man was looking through stuff in here and he pointed it out to me. I thought you might like it for your cards."

I snorted. "I couldn't fit all my cards in there!"

"I know *that*. But when you go to shows and swaps and stuff it would be good for carrying the best ones."

She was right, but I didn't want to admit it too quickly. So I picked up the box and looked it over. The polished wood had a reddish color, and when I rubbed it, it gave off a kind of spicy odor. It was pretty nice.

"It's locked," I said, wrinkling my brow.

"So? You can take care of that."

Sometimes I get the impression Sarah thinks I can do anything—which is nice, but also a little nerve-racking, since I don't want to do anything that would show I can't. In this case she was probably right; I could find some way to open the box.

"It doesn't have a price tag," I said disapprovingly.

Sarah rolled her eyes. "So go ask how much they want for it! It probably won't be that much. And remember, you don't have to pay what they ask for the first time. People *always* make deals at this kind of sale."

"I know that!" I said. (Which was true, if you considered that I knew it now that she had said it. I figured Sarah was probably right, since she had been to enough garage sales with my mother that she should be an expert by now.)

I looked at the box for a minute longer. Then, mostly to put off making a decision, I suggested that we go look at some other stuff. I hid the box under the desk before we left the room, so no one would buy it while I was making up my mind.

Going off to look at other stuff was fine with Sarah; she loves that kind of old junk. But I couldn't stop thinking about the box, and after a few minutes I went back to examine it again.

Finally I took it to the woman sitting at the card table in the front room.

"So—how much do you want for this dumb box?" I asked, trying to sound cool.

She took it from my hands, studied it for a moment, then said, "Five dollars."

I could feel my eyes bulge, but I tried not to make a choking sound. "How about a dollar?"

The woman laughed out loud. I started to blush.

"Two dollars?" I asked.

"Four," she replied.

Well, that was progress. Maybe Sarah was right.

"How about two fifty?" I suggested. As I did, I noticed something weird: Now that I had started to try to buy the box, I *really* wanted it.

The woman narrowed her eyes. "Three fifty," she said in a firm voice.

And that was as low as she would go. Which was a lot better than five, but still a problem, since I only had two dollars and thirty seven cents in my pocket. (When I realized *that*, I was actually relieved that she hadn't said yes to my offer of two fifty. I would have looked really stupid counting out the change and coming up thirteen cents short after all that bargaining.)

I thought about going home and trying to hit up my grandmother for some money. But I was afraid someone would buy the box while I was gone, even if I hid it again.

So I went to see if I could get a loan from Sarah.

She was in one of the bedrooms, trying on old hats. "Do you like this?" she asked when I came into the room. She was wearing something blue and fuzzy. It didn't look bad on her.

"It looks stupid," I said, just like I always did when she asked if I liked something.

She made a face. "Don't be such a snot."

She was right. I shouldn't be a snot if I wanted to borrow money from her. She noticed I was carrying the box. "Did you buy it?" she asked, looking pleased.

I shook my head. "I don't have enough money. How much do you have?"

She looked nervous.

"I'll pay you back," I said, exasperated.

"You still owe me a dollar from last week."

"I've got it at home. You just never asked for it."

"I did too!"

"Look, all I need is a dollar and thirteen cents."

She frowned. "I want to buy this hat."

The hat was a dollar fifty. Sarah had two dollars. I felt like I was trapped in a math problem.

"Let's see if we can make a deal," said Sarah.

The woman didn't look exactly pleased to see me, so I let Sarah do the talking. Having a cute little sister is not always a bad thing. She twinkled and pleaded and pouted, and next thing I knew, the woman had sold us both the hat and the box for four dollars and thirty cents.

We argued all the way home about how much I owed Sarah.

The argument stopped when we walked through the front door and Mr. Perkins bit me.

II. Monkey Business

Mr. Perkins is my mother's monkey. Mom got him last year when she turned forty. She said she had always wanted a monkey when she was a kid, but her parents wouldn't let her have one. Now she was going to have one no matter what anyone thought.

What I thought was that it would be cool to have a monkey. That was before we actually got Mr. Perkins and I found out how loud, smelly, and cranky monkeys really are. Also that they like to pee on your head, which he has done twice to me.

Anyway, Mr. Perkins bit me when we came through the door. I yelled and dropped the box. Mr. Perkins grabbed it and ran away. Sarah and I chased him around the house, making so much noise that after a while Gramma Walker heard and came to help us. (She's very deaf.) We cornered the monkey behind my father's reading chair, and I finally managed to get the box back.

(Gramma Walker is my father's mother, by the way. My mother's mother won't visit us now that Mom has the monkey. She takes it personally.)

The only good thing about all the fuss was that by the time it was over Sarah gave up bugging me about how much money I owed her—probably because she could tell I was in such a totally bad mood it wouldn't do her any good.

I took the box into my room and slammed the door behind me. Then I got out the tiny screwdrivers my Grampa Hartz had given me for my birthday and started working on the box.

It wasn't easy; I ended up taking the hinges right off, and the darn thing still wouldn't open until I poked the littlest screwdriver in between the lid and the body of the box and pried them apart.

Something like sparkling fog came pouring over the edge. A blue glow showed through the opening. A crackle of tingling energy shot through my fingers.

"Yow!" I cried.

When I let go of the lid, it slammed back onto the body of the box so fast it was almost as if it had been sucked down.

I stared at the box for several minutes. When I finally got up enough courage, I reached forward and touched it again, just a little tap with the tip of my finger.

9

I pulled my hand back quickly.

Nothing happened.

I tried again.

Still nothing.

Must have been some weird buildup of static electricity, I told myself. But I wasn't entirely convinced, and I was plenty nervous when I reached forward to open the box. Only I couldn't resist.

The lid creaked as I pried it open. On its underside, painted in fancy letters, were the words MARTIN MORLEY'S LITTLE MONSTERS.

Below that, in very fine print, it said, "Let whosoever opens this box do so with good heart, lest my curse fall upon him."

"Yeah, right," I muttered. It looked as if Old Man Morley was even kookier than everyone had thought.

The box was divided into five compartments. Inside each compartment was a statue of a tiny monster. Three appeared to be male, two female. They were very detailed, beautifully made, and extremely weird.

At the base of each compartment was an engraved nameplate. I had to rub them with a tissue before I could read them.

I blinked. According to the nameplates, the monsters' names were Gaspar, Albert, Darlene, Marie, and Bob.

"Weird names for a bunch of monsters," I

muttered as I picked up Gaspar. (At least, I assumed he was Gaspar. It was always possible someone had played with the monsters and then put them back in the wrong slots.)

The little monster was about five inches tall. He had a head like a lizard's stuck on top of a muscular, manlike body. A spiny crest rose from the top of his head, and a long, powerful tail extended from the back of his ragged trousers. He looked (and felt) as if he were made of solid brass. I fooled around with him a little, making him bounce across my desk and growl and stuff. Then I stood him at the edge of the box and took out the next figurine.

Albert was a typical mad scientist's assistant—a fierce-looking hunchback with shaggy hair and a squinty face. His hands stretched forward in a grabbing gesture, as if he had been frozen in mid-action. Whoever had made him was really good. He even had a patch sewed into the back of his coarse tunic to make room for his hump. It was all done in brass, of course. But the effect was very realistic.

Still holding Albert, I looked at the others. Darlene was sort of a vampire lady. She had a long cape wrapped around her, big eyes, and a pair of fangs that poked down over her lower lip. Marie had snakes for hair. Bob looked like your basic wolfman. With all of them, the detail work was amazing; Marie's face, for example, had tiny, delicate scales. I began to wonder if the figurines might be more valuable than I had expected.

I was about to set Albert next to Gaspar so I could pick up another one when Sarah shrieked, "Anthony! *Help!*"

Her voice was coming from the bathroom. Still holding Albert, I pushed away from my desk and raced down the hall.

The bathroom door was half open. From inside I could hear running water and angry chattering. I groaned. Sarah was trying to give Mr. Perkins a bath again.

The floor was like a swamp. Mr. Perkins, soaking wet, clung to my sister's neck, screeching and hissing. Sarah was half soaked herself, and her damp hair lay flat on her forehead.

"You get back in that tub!" she ordered the monkey as I came through the door. She was struggling to pull him from her neck. He was struggling to hold on.

What really griped me was that he didn't bite her, and probably wouldn't, no matter how upset he got. Me he bites out of sheer cussedness. My pukey little sister could tie his tail around her neck, and he still wouldn't set tooth in her skin.

"Anthony!" cried Sarah again. *"Help!"*

What did she expect me to do? If I got near the monkey he was sure to take a chunk out of me. I set Albert on the back of the toilet and made a couple of moves as if to help Sarah, but my heart wasn't in it. It didn't matter. A minute later she had Mr. Perkins off her neck and back in the bathtub.

It was like turning on a blender. Water splashed all over the place.

When we were finally done with Mr. Perkins, I noticed that some water had splashed onto Albert's hand. When I said something about it, Sarah noticed the little monster for the first time. I ended up showing her the whole set, which she thought was pretty cool.

I didn't think anything more about Albert's hand until a few hours after supper (Gramma Walker's prize-winning beef stew), when I decided to take a last look at my monsters before I went to sleep. Then I saw that his hand had changed color, the brass tones transformed to a dark, fleshy shade.

I got mad, because I figured the water had damaged whatever Albert was made of. But when I touched his hand, I drew my finger back quickly, my anger transformed to fear.

The little monster's hand was no longer cold and metallic. It now felt warm; warm and . . . fleshy.

I picked up the little statue and stared at it. Its fingers began to move.

III. Hand Made

I slapped Albert back in the box, closed the lid, and latched it. Then I put the box in the bottom drawer of my desk, closed the drawer, and locked that, too.

But I didn't leave it there. I couldn't.

Which isn't to say I didn't try. But I couldn't sleep, thinking about that tiny hand, stretching and grasping. It was horrifying—but not as horrible as the thought that a living creature was locked, frozen, in my desk. A creature I could revive just by adding water.

The idea of keeping him frozen (or statued, or whatever) was too awful. Unfortunately, the idea of bringing him completely to life was pretty awful as well. I mean, what kind of monster was he?

Well, a small one, to begin with. It wasn't like he could rip my head off or anything.

After an hour or so of this fussing I got out of bed and went to my desk. I took out the box and opened it. Albert's fist was still moving, clenching and unclenching, a bit of living flesh stuck on a lifeless metallic figurine.

"All right, buddy," I whispered. "Let's thaw you out."

I started down the hall, then stopped and went back to my sister's room. I stood outside her door, trying to decide whether to wake her. Part of me wanted to do this on my own, keep it all to myself. Another part of me thought it would be a good idea to have someone else along, just in case things got out of hand— and so I would have someone to talk to about it.

Finally I knocked on the door, then pushed it open and hissed, "Hey, Sarah! Wake up!"

She moaned. "What do you want, Anthony?" (She doesn't like waking up, especially in the middle of the night.)

"I have to show you something."

She sat up fast, and I remembered that the last time I'd woken her and said that, I had also shoved a snake into her bed.

"This is different," I said urgently. I turned on the lamp next to her bed as I spoke, then thrust Albert into the cone of light.

Sarah gasped at the sight of the moving fingers. Scrooching back against the wall, she whispered, "Anthony, that is *too* weird." She shuddered. "How did you do it?"

"It happened when he got wet. I'm going to go get the rest of him wet now."

Sarah grabbed my arm. "Do you think you should?"

"I have to. It's not right to leave him like this."

"Maybe he's that way for a reason," said Sarah, who is very big on being sensible. "Maybe he's *evil*."

"Maybe whoever froze him was evil."

Sarah thought about that for a moment. Though she's big on being sensible, she's also big on compassion. She'll probably be a vegetarian in a year or so. "How can we find out?" she whispered at last.

"Unfreeze him."

She made a face. "But what if it turns out that he *is* evil?"

"We'll squash him!"

I said that with more certainty than I actually felt, and I had a brief vision of Albert escaping and hiding in the walls, then sneaking out at night to torment us. But just as I was about to change my mind, Sarah said, "Okay, let's do it!"

She slipped out of bed and grabbed a flashlight from her nightstand. We were both supposed to have flashlights, but I had lost mine.

We tiptoed down the hallway—though we didn't really need to since Gramma Walker is so hard of hearing that we probably could have stomped to the bathroom without waking her up. In the glow of the flashlight I could see Albert's tiny hand, stretching and grasping.

"What do we do now?" asked Sarah when we got to the bathroom.

"Get him wet," I replied. I looked at him for a second, then added, "Do you think we should sprinkle him, or dunk him?"

Sarah thought for a moment. "Dunk him," she said at last. "It would be really gross if he came to life in little spots all over his body. It might be dangerous, too. I mean for him."

I wasn't sure what the medical rules were for bringing a monster back to life. But I decided Sarah was right.

So we filled the sink. I meant to dip Albert into the water and then pull him out. But as soon as I put him in, the water began to bubble and boil, splashing over the edge of the sink like some sort of weird chemical reaction. I dropped Albert and jumped back with a yelp. Sarah huddled against me.

When the water calmed down, I saw a little hand come thrusting through the surface.

"He's drowning!" hissed Sarah. "Go save him, Anthony!"

I started forward, but Albert was already hauling himself onto the edge of the sink. He shook his head, spattering tiny drops of water in all directions. Then he stood, stretched his arms, threw his head back, and growled.

It was a tiny sound, but terrifying nonetheless.

He walked along the edge of the basin, looking puzzled. "What a strange white road," he muttered.

I cleared my throat. Albert glanced up at me and Sarah.

"*Monsters!*" he screamed. Then he dove back into the sink.

I walked over and looked in. Albert was at the bottom of the basin, clinging to the drain plug. I didn't do anything at first, but when I began to be afraid he might drown, I reached in and pulled him out. He pounded on my fingers as I lifted him. I half expected him to bite me, too, but that was probably only because I've spent so much time with Mr. Perkins.

Albert didn't bite. He just squirmed like a demented squirrel, shouting, "Let me go, you big brute!"

"Hey, hey," I said softly, "I'm not going to hurt you. I thawed you out, didn't I?"

He blinked, and a series of expressions raced across his face, shifting through surprise, understanding, anger, fear, and back to understanding. "Uh-oh," he said. "I think we've got a little problem here." Looking up at me, he asked in a suspicious voice: "What are you, anyway?"

"I'm a kid."

His eyes got wider. "How did you get so big?" he asked, sounding both awed and nervous.

"How'd you get so small?" I responded.

We stared at each other for a moment. As far as I was concerned, I wasn't all that big. Heck, if I was, I wouldn't have so many problems with Ralph Mangram at school. But I was certainly big compared to Albert. At first I had figured that the little guy had somehow gotten shrunk. But suddenly I wondered if maybe he was from some other world. Maybe he had always been this tiny, and we humans were giants compared to his people!

"Would you put me down, please?" he asked softly.

I set him on the edge of the sink, then knelt so that we were face-to-face.

His head was about the size of my eyeball.

Sarah knelt next to me.

"So, where are you from?" I asked.

"Transylvania, originally," said Albert.

Well, that was on Earth. So much for the other world theory.

Sounding nervous, Albert asked, "Where am I now?"

"Owl's Roost, Nebraska," said Sarah proudly.

Albert's eyes widened. "But that's where I live!" He swallowed. "You're not really giants, are you?"

Sarah and I shook our heads.

Albert sat down, cross-legged, his shoulders drooping, his hump nearly as high as his head.

"I've been shrunk!" he moaned. He sounded really depressed. I suppose you couldn't blame him. Suddenly he jumped to his feet. "Where are the others?"

"In the box," I replied.

"The box?!?"

"The box you came in," explained Sarah.

"Well, go get them! Then we have to figure out a way to get back to our normal size." He looked around, then said, "Wait a minute. What year is this? It *is* 1941 . . . isn't it?"

From the tone of his voice I could tell he had a pretty good idea that it *wasn't* 1941. But when I told him he was off by more than fifty years, he screamed.

"Martin did this! Oh, I knew he was up to no good. Come on, we *have* to wake up the others!"

"What's the hurry?" I asked, still not sure I wanted to unthaw all five little monsters.

Albert leaped from the sink, grabbed the front of my pajamas, and scrambled up my chest like a sailor climbing a ship's rigging. I jumped backward and tried to brush him off, but he was too strong. Once he had reached my shoulder, he stuck his head in my ear and bellowed, "The hurry is, they're my family and I don't want them frozen! Besides, I'm not the smart one. We need Gaspar and Darlene. *Now, go get them!"*

Jeez. And I had thought Mr. Perkins was a problem.

We started down the hall to get the other monsters, Albert riding in the big pocket on the left side of my bathrobe. Sarah positioned herself on the other side of me, then tugged my sleeve and whispered, "Anthony, do you think this is a good idea?"

"It's probably a terrible idea. But it's the most interesting thing we've ever done. Besides, I don't think we could talk Albert out of it. And even if we could . . ."

Sarah nodded as my voice trailed off. I sensed that, like me, she was thinking about the little monsters having been frozen (or whatever) for over fifty years. It was time to disenchant them.

When we got to my room, I set Albert on my desk. He ran to the box. "Boss!" he cried in horror when he saw Gaspar. "Oh, Boss, what has that maniac done to you?"

"I take it he didn't always look like that?" I asked, picking up the lizard-headed monster.

"I'm not worried about how he looks, you idiot," Albert said. "We can change that. It's the fact that he's been shrunk and turned into a statue that has me upset." He walked along the front of the box, gazing into each compartment. "Poor Marie," he sighed. "Poor Darlene. Asleep for over half a century."

"Not what you'd call sleeping beauties," I remarked.

"Beauty is as beauty does," snapped Albert. He stopped in front of the last slot, the one with the wolfman-type guy. "Alas, poor Bob," he said, patting the figurine. "Stuck in this horrible form all these years."

"So Bob didn't always look like that, either?" asked Sarah.

Albert shook his head. "Only occasionally. He's were."

"Were what?" I asked. Then I got it. "Oh! You mean he's a werewolf?"

"Not quite," said Albert. "Come on, let's stop talking and wake them up."

I put Gaspar back in the box. With Albert on my shoulder I headed back to the bathroom.

It was monster time.

IV. Midnight Trip to Morley Manor

If putting Albert in the sink had made it seem like we had started a chemical reaction, this time it was as if the sink had turned into a volcano. The thing just about erupted. Water sprayed everywhere, coming out so forcefully it hit the ceiling.

A minute later four coughing, gagging little monsters climbed out of the sink. They were wet, bedraggled, and extremely confused. But they were also overjoyed to see one another.

"Marie!" shouted Darlene.

"Darlene!" shouted Marie.

They threw their arms around each other and hugged. Then Marie looked up and spotted me and Sarah.

Her scream was amazingly loud for someone so tiny.

The other monsters looked up. Their eyes went wide and they cowered together—except for Gaspar, the lizard-headed guy. He just closed his eyes and heaved a deep sigh.

Despite Albert's attempts to assure the group that Sarah and I were friendly, it took several minutes for them to settle down. When they finally did, Albert introduced first Sarah, then me, and explained that we had been the ones to disenchant them.

When Albert was done, Gaspar made a deep bow. In a hissy voice, with his long tongue flickering in and out, he said, "My deepest thanks to you for releasing me and my family from bondage."

Albert had said something about family, too.

"So you guys are all, like, related?" I asked.

Gaspar smiled—which was somewhat terrifying, given how many teeth he had. "Well, Albert isn't actually family—though he has worked for me for so long that it often feels as if he is. But Darlene and Marie are my sisters. And Bob is our faithful dog."

"Dog?" cried Sarah. "I thought he was a werewolf!"

Gaspar actually laughed, a harsh hacking sound. "Bob is a were-*human*. Most of the time he's a cocker spaniel, but on full-moon nights he turns into something sort of like a human being. It's very frightening for him."

Bob whined in agreement.

Gaspar tapped the end of his long face and said, "Hmmm. Must be a full moon tonight, as well, or Bob would have turned back. At least, I think he would. It's hard to say how what we have been through would affect his condition."

"So, how did you get so small?" I asked.

Gaspar's eyes grew wide. "Treachery!" he replied, with something like a snarl. "Foul treachery. It was the work of my brother, Martin. He was the one who shrunk us."

"Did he turn you into monsters, too?" I asked.

"Oh, no!" hissed Marie, the words coming from the snakes on her head rather than from her mouth. "We did that oursssselvesss! Only we don't like the word *monsterssss*. We prefer to ssssay we are . . . *sssspecial*."

"You *wanted* to be mons—er . . . special?" asked Sarah in astonishment.

Darlene smiled, showing her fangs. "Vell, it seemed like a good idea at the time. Ve vere not planning on making it . . . permanent."

Her accent reminded me of Bela Lugosi in the movie *Dracula*. Since none of the others had that accent, and since she was supposed to be their sister, I wondered if she was faking it. Or maybe it had come with the transformation that had made her a vampire to begin with.

Bob sat down and tried to scratch behind his ear with his foot. He couldn't quite manage it, though.

Darlene patted his head sympathetically.

"Do you know where our enemy is?" asked Gaspar. His forked tongue flickered between his thin lips like red lightning.

Albert tugged at his lab coat. "Boss, there's something you need to know."

"What?" asked Gaspar impatiently.

"We've been sleeping for over fifty years!"

Gaspar threw back his head and hissed in rage. He tightened his fists and waved them at the ceiling. His thick tail thrashed back and forth. It was all very dramatic, if somewhat tiny. Finally he dropped his hands to his side. Chest heaving, he said, "Does Martin still live?"

"Not if he's the guy we used to call 'Old Man Morley,' " I replied. "He died last month."

Gaspar hissed again. "We must get back to the house as soon as possible."

"Why?" asked Sarah.

"It isss the only way for ussss to get back to our own ssssizzzze," hissed the snakes on Marie's head, writhing in agitation.

"The *only* way?" I asked nervously.

"Absolutely," said Gaspar. He sounded desperate. "Everything we need is in my laboratory—both the scientific equipment and the materials for our spells."

"You use science *and* magic?" asked Sarah.

"Vy does that surprize you?" asked Darlene, showing her fangs.

Sarah shrugged. "I don't know. It just seems weird."

I knew what she meant. In the books I read they always use either science *or* magic to do stuff, but not both. When I mentioned that, Gaspar replied, "It is a small view of the world. People always do that, put things in compartments. It's like thinking that an artist should either paint pictures or make statues, but not both. But what's to say you can't combine things? The ancient Greeks used to paint their statues."

"Are you sure about that?" I asked. "I've seen pictures of those statues. They didn't look painted to me."

"It wore off," hissed Gaspar, his tongue flickering over his teeth. "The point is, you should not limit your possibilities."

"Actually," put in Albert, "the main point is, we have to get back to the house if we're going to get back to our regular size."

I glanced at Sarah. "I'm afraid there's a small problem," I said, my voice nearly a whisper.

"What?" asked Gaspar sharply.

I swallowed. "They're going to start tearing the place down tomorrow morning!"

All five little monsters began to carry on something awful. Marie's snakes had a hissy fit. Darlene turned into an inch-long bat and began fluttering around like a moth at a candle. Albert stomped around, wailing and beating his chest like Tarzan. Gaspar put his arm to his brow like some tragic hero. And Bob threw back his head and howled a tiny howl.

"Oh, stop!" said Sarah at last. "If it's that important we'll take you back tonight."

"We will?" I asked in surprise.

"We have to," said Sarah, her voice urgent. I realized she was right. It was the monsters' only chance to get back to their regular size.

On the other hand, I wasn't sure that was such a good idea. I mean, did we really want five full-sized monsters running around Owl's Roost?

As if he had read my mind, Gaspar said, "Not only is it the only way for us to return to our regular size, it is the only way for us to return home."

"I thought this was where you lived. I mean, here in Owls' Roost. Or do you mean back to your own time?"

"Our other home," hissed Marie's snakes. "Through the Sssstarry Door."

"What's the Starry Door?" asked Sarah.

"Never mind that now," snapped Gaspar, shooting Marie a dark look. "The point is, if we don't get back to the house before they tear it down, we'll be stuck here."

"And ve vill haf to stay vit you," added Darlene.

Well, that settled it as far as I was concerned. While it might be cool to have the monsters around for a while, I sure didn't want it to be a permanent situation. I could already tell they would be more trouble than they were worth.

The thing was, I was still a little nervous about what might happen when they got back to full size.

"Uh—if we take you back and help you get big, you won't eat us, or tear us limb from limb, or anything like that, will you?" I asked nervously.

Gaspar was outraged. "What kind of people do you think we are?"

I spread my hands. "I don't have the slightest idea!"

Darlene put a hand on Gaspar's shoulder and

whispered in his ear. I could see him relax a little. Turning to me, he said, "My apologies for my outburst. Your concern is not unfounded. Let us see if we can reduce it a bit. Family! Assemble!"

Quickly all five monsters got in a line. Placing his clenched fist over his heart, Gaspar said, "In return for your assistance, we pledge you our friendship, our support in time of need, our sacred honor, and our hope for a better tomorrow. Thus speaks the Family Morleskievich!"

"Thus speaks the family Morleskievich!" shouted the rest of them (well, all except Bob).

Then all five of them made a deep bow in our direction.

"Morleskievich?" asked Sarah.

"Our name before we came to America," said Gaspar. "We only use it for our most serious oaths."

Well, they could have been lying. But we decided to believe them.

"Do you think we should wake up Gramma?" asked Sarah as we got ready to leave.

I made my *yeah, right!* face at her, and she nodded. "I guess not," she said. But I don't want to go alone."

"Don't worry," I replied, trying to sound braver than I felt. "It's not like anyone lives there now."

"I wouldn't count on that," muttered Gaspar.

"What's that supposed to mean?" I asked sharply.

He shrugged and said, "The world is vast and strange, dear boy. The world is vast and strange."

"Yeah," I said, "and getting stranger by the minute."

Fifteen minutes later Sarah and I were dressed and heading out the back door. The clock in the kitchen said 11:45. Gramma Walker was still snoring in her bedroom.

Though the rain had stopped, it appeared to be a temporary situation. Dark clouds hid any sign of the stars and moon, and thunder rumbled ominously in the distance.

"So much for finding out whether Bob should have returned to his own shape or not," muttered Gaspar.

Sarah and I had divided the monsters between us. Albert was in my right pocket, Bob in my left. Darlene and Marie were riding with Sarah. And Gaspar was sitting on the collar of my raincoat, clinging to my ear. It felt a little weird, but it let him talk to me. As we slogged through the wet streets, he began telling me his story, shouting a bit so that Sarah could hear it, too.

"I was born in Transylvania," he began, "nearly a century ago. I was the second of a set of twin boys. My brother, Martin, beat me into the world by thirteen minutes and thirteen seconds.

"Martin and I were identical, not only in face but in feeling. Our minds and our hearts were as one. We thought the same thoughts, felt the same feelings. And the thing we felt most strongly of all was curiosity.

"In the summer of our twelfth year—both our sisters had been born by then, though Darlene was still but a toddler—Martin and I scaled the wall of the haunted castle that stood a mile from our village. Inside, we found a great secret. The castle was indeed haunted by the ghosts of its former residents. But there was someone else there as well—someone neither living nor dead."

"Who?" asked Sarah eagerly.

"A wizard named Wentar. He wandered the castle halls as penance for his misdeeds. At least, that was what we believed at the time. I have since learned better.

"Had either Martin or I been alone when we met Wentar, we probably would have fled in horror the moment we saw him. But being together gave us courage. So we challenged the wizard."

Gaspar stopped speaking for a moment and stared into the rain, as if remembering something. Finally he shuddered—I could feel it in my neck—and went on with his story.

"Wentar asked our aid in freeing his soul from its curse, and we were glad to give it, though the task he assigned us turned out to be more terrifying than we could have imagined."

"What was it?" I asked.

"It's a long and horrible story, and I don't have time to tell you right now. The point is, as a reward for doing this, Wentar showed us the secret entrance to his chamber, where there was hidden such a store of forbidden knowledge as I can hardly tell you."

He sighed. "Well, there is a reason much of that knowledge is forbidden. Soon Martin and I were tampering and toying with forces far beyond our understanding, walking an edge of danger that we barely understood. Then one day Martin fell through a hole in the world.

"I was terrified. Should I go after him? Wait for him? Run for help?

"Before I could decide what to do, Martin returned. He was Martin—yet not Martin. Something about him was different. His spirit was darker. Sorrow colored his eyes. He would no longer speak to me as freely as he once had. And of what had happened, where he had been, he would not speak at all.

"Yet despite this horrifying experience, we did not cease our visits to the castle. If anything, Martin was more eager than ever to continue our investigations. Years went by. We grew stronger and bolder in our knowledge. Then, in the late 1930s, Martin decided that we should all move to America. Our parents were dead by that time, so by 'all' I mean our two sisters, Martin and myself, and Albert.

" 'Something terrible is coming,' Martin kept saying, 'An evil almost beyond imagination.' "

Gaspar fell silent, and I could sense that he was fighting back some painful feelings. He was about to continue his story when we reached the gate to Morley Manor.

"Home!" he hissed, in a voice that carried more anger and joy and loss and sorrow than I had ever heard put into a single word before.

I still had a million questions. But Gaspar wasn't answering. His attention was focused on only one thing now: getting big again.

V. Magnified Monsters

The gate to Morley Manor was about twelve feet tall, with fierce spikes on the top. I was afraid it would be locked, but I guess the owners figured that since the place was going to be torn down there was no point in keeping people out. Or maybe they just figured that no one with a brain in his head would want to go in there anyway.

The hinges were so badly rusted that Sarah and I both had to push the gate to get it open. It creaked loudly as it went. The rain was starting again, and of course we couldn't hold our umbrellas while we were pushing. My head was soaked by the time we were done, and I wished that I had bothered to put up the hood on my raincoat. Gaspar was soaked, too, so at least I wasn't alone. Bob and Albert, on the other hand, ducked into my pockets and closed the flaps. So they stayed dry. It was weird to feel them moving around, almost as if I had a hamster in each pocket.

A streak of lightning crackled through the sky as we started up the walk. Thunder boomed and crashed around us. I expected Sarah to say she wanted to go home, but she didn't. The weird thing was, I think having the monsters with us made us both feel braver. I mean, this place was very spooky, but we were on their side, and the place seemed sort of natural for them.

The front door was unlocked, too. As we stepped inside a clock began to strike midnight.

"That's weird," said Sarah nervously.

"What?" I asked, barely able to get the word past the dryness in my throat.

"There aren't any clocks here. I watched a lady buy them all this morning."

I shivered.

We decided to take off our raincoats. First we let the monsters out of our pockets. Marie started to cry when she saw the terrible condition of the house. The snakes on her head drooped and fell flat about her shoulders.

The furniture was almost all gone—sold or hauled away. But we found a rickety table where we could set the monsters.

Sarah and I knelt in front of it so we could talk to them.

"What next?" I whispered.

"We climb the forbidden stair," said Gaspar.

"I should have guessed," I muttered. "All right, where is it?" Remembering the roped-off stair I had seen that morning, I said, "Never mind, I think I know. You guys wanna walk or ride?"

They decided to walk, so we put them gently on the floor—except for Darlene, who turned back into a bat, and flew instead.

The sign saying Absolutely No One Admitted Past This Point was still in place. "What's up there?" I asked when we stood at the base of the stairs.

"My laboratory," said Gaspar. "At least, I hope it's still there." He sounded both happy and slightly nervous.

"And the Sssstarry Door," hissed Marie's snakes.

The stairs were too high for the monsters to

climb, so Sarah and I picked them up again. Swallowing hard, we started toward the top. Suddenly something crashed below us, so loud and hard that it nearly sent my heart flying out of my chest.

"What was that?" screamed Sarah.

"Just the house," said Gaspar. When it was clear that we didn't understand, he added, "It makes sounds all by itself."

I could feel my eyes bulge. "What's *that* supposed to mean?"

"Just don't open any doors vithout asking us first," whispered Darlene, who was driving me nuts by fluttering around a few inches from my head.

I was thinking about turning back. Then Bob growled from inside my pocket, and I decided we should probably keep climbing.

Of course, we could have just ditched the little monsters and run for home. But they knew where we lived, and I had a feeling they would have been back. If we could help them get big again, maybe they would just go through the "Starry Door" (whatever that was) and leave us alone.

Even so, I could feel my feet dragging as we approached the top of the stairs.

A cold wind came whistling down past us, as if someone had suddenly opened an upstairs window.

Sarah shivered. "Where did that come from?"

"It's the house," said Gaspar again.

"Maybe you guys should go the rest of the way on your own," I suggested, stopping a few feet from the top.

"We can't open the laboratory door when we're only five inches high!" hissed Marie, sounding as if she thought I was some sort of idiot for suggesting that.

I sighed and walked on. All too soon we were at the top of the stairs.

A long hallway stretched ahead of us.

Ridiculously long.

Impossibly long, when you came right down to it. That is, it was clear that the hallway went on a lot longer than the house did. Somewhere along there the house stopped, at least if you were standing outside. But inside, the hall just kept on going.

What was at the end of it?

"We need to go through the third door on the right," said Gaspar.

The floor creaked beneath our feet.

The door creaked as I pushed it open.

By the light of Sarah's flashlight we could see what looked like a mad scientist's laboratory crossed with a wizard's hideaway. Medical tables stood side by side with tall wooden stands on which lay thick, ancient books. The shelves held test tubes and beakers, as well as green glass bottles with labels like EYE OF NEWT and POWDERED BAT WING. Dust lay thick over everything. Cobwebs stretched from the ceiling to the floor.

One shelf had been overturned. The room looked as if no one had entered it in fifty years.

On the far side of the room stood five glass chambers.

"Thank goodness they're still here," said Gaspar when he spotted the chambers. "That's where we need to go to be enlarged." Turning to me, he said, "You will have to operate the controls for us."

"What are you going to use for power?" I asked. "The electricity has been cut off."

"We don't have to fly kites to catch lightning or anything, do we?" asked Sarah nervously.

Gaspar laughed. "There are many other sources of power in this world," he said. Then he directed me to a metal box that lay on a table near the center of the room. The box had a glass top, and through a layer of dust and cobwebs I could see that it held an enormous green jewel.

"This is the Heart of Wentar," he said.

"The *what?*" I cried.

"It's not his real heart," said Gaspar, sounding exasperated. "At least, not anymore. Place it in the control box over there."

Nervously I brushed aside the cobwebs and took the jewel from the box. Though it was as smooth as glass, it seemed to pulse with energy.

The monsters were getting excited.

"Now throw this switch," said Gaspar.

I glanced at Sarah. She nodded. I pulled the switch. The five glass chambers rose into the air.

The monsters scurried across the floor and took their places, one in each chamber.

At Gaspar's direction I pulled the switch back. The chambers descended again. Then I pressed three buttons he had shown me, in the exact order he had indicated.

A green mist began to fill the chambers. At the same time the storm broke out in full fury again. Thunder shook the sky outside. Rain pounded against the roof.

Suddenly a crackle of energy filled the room, so strong and intense that Sarah and I both cried out, and when I reached for her hand, a bolt of green power shot between us.

I could see the monsters getting bigger, slowly at first, then faster and faster until they were taller than us.

Gaspar howled in triumph.

The glass chambers lifted.

"Big!" he cried in a deep baritone voice. "We're big again!"

Albert leaped from the chamber and began to caper about the room, snorting with delight.

Darlene swirled her cape and transformed herself into a bat that had a wingspan of at least three feet. Marie's snakes were so excited they nearly tied themselves into knots. Bob threw back his head and howled with joy.

"Ah, my young friends, the Family Morleskievich is deeply in your debt," said Gaspar, stepping toward me.

I know he meant to be friendly, but now that he was over six feet high, his lizard head was terrifying. I took a step backward.

Gaspar stopped, and smiled, showing about four thousand teeth. "I understand your reluctance for me to approach," he said. "Very well. We will be on our way."

The five monsters gathered at the door. "You have done the family Morleskievich a great favor," said Gaspar. "We thank you." Then they all made the same sweeping bow they had made when they pledged us their friendship.

I felt a little sad when they opened the door to leave. But proud, too. We had helped the monsters.

My sorrow and pride lasted until Gaspar opened the door and we saw who was waiting on the other side.

TO BE CONTINUED IN
BRUCE COVILLE'S BOOK OF ALIENS II

Every kid knows that the first day of a new school year can be a terrifying experience. Heck, sometimes just getting there is more than you can handle. . . .

THE FIRST EXCUSE

Nina Kiriki Hoffman

So it's the first day of sixth grade and I'm waiting on the corner like always for the bus, my lunch in a dumb brown paper bag. No, Mom would not get me that new lunchbox with Griffin O'Reilly and the Meltdowns on it or even a thermos. I have to use a brown paper bag and drink out of a dumb box that doesn't even keep the grape drink cold.

Anyway, the bus is coming and I'm worrying for the fifteenth time that morning if *this* white shirt covered with big turquoise blue flowers and *these* rainbow-striped shorts and *these* black-court hightops with the neon-blue lightning bolts are the right things to wear to school on the first day of a new year when you

want to change into someone else instead of the dorkette you were last year, when it hits me.

The bus is the wrong color yellow.

I mean, there are a lot of things I don't know—who can listen to teachers all the time? Especially if you just got six new colored pencils with your allowance and they're crying to be used and one of them is the perfect, the absolute perfect color for robots, my favorite thing to draw? So I'm not too sure about spelling some of the longer and more ridiculous words, ones that don't make sense, like using *gh* to spell *f*—whose dumb idea was that? Wouldn't it make more sense to spell it *enuff?* Like, you know, *stuff?* And sometimes you spell it *threw*, which works because it's like *ewww*, and sometimes the *gh* is silent, like in *through*. Who came up with this dumb system?

And then there's fractions. I dare you to tell me which part multiplies which part when you're doing this fraction times a fraction thing. As far as I can tell it switches back and forth whenever the teacher wants it to.

None of that stuff makes much sense to me. But I do know colors.

You've got to know what color a school bus is. They don't change.

This bus was banana-colored, not the darker,

more orangey Garfield-the-Cat color a bus should be.

Once I noticed the color of the bus, I noticed a few other things. Like its front bumper was smiling. Not just a straight flat chrome line. This bumper was full out smiling like some car in a cartoon.

Also the front windshield wasn't clean and clear. It was foggy. I couldn't quite make out anything through the window. There was a dark person-shaped object where the driver should be, but how could he or she see out through all that dirty, frosty muck on the window? I *mean.* Other considerations aside, potential safety hazard right there.

So the bus pulls up next to me and the door opens, only it doesn't make the right noise. No *swish-whoosh,* or *clankety-crank,* just this little popping sound. Like a mouth opening.

It smelled the way your mouth tastes ten minutes after you finish a glass of milk.

Looking inside, I could see the stairs weren't really stairs. They were more like a ramp. A ramp covered with juicy bumps. You ever look at your tongue through a magnifying glass? Everybody knows buses have black rubber on the floor, not pink furry juicy stuff.

That dark shape in the driver's seat? Well, what driver's seat? It looked more like something or someone kind of welded to the floor of the bus. Or maybe like a giant black fang sticking up out of this pink juicy bumpy stuff.

All the side windows were cloudy, too. And they were the wrong shape. Round, like eyes, but without eyeballs. I couldn't see anybody through them. Not even anybody that looked like a big black tooth, you know? Nothing moved behind those windows.

My stop has never been the first one on the route. Usually there's a bunch of kids on the bus before it gets to my stop.

I ask you. Would you have gotten onto that bus?

I really like the first day of school. Honest. Nobody makes you do much work and you get to check out all the other kids and what's happened to their bodies over the summer, and whether anybody else has fashion sense. I didn't want to miss it.

But given a choice between being eaten by a bus and running, well, you know.

I spent the whole day hiding in the tree house in the Schwabs' backyard. Luckily I hung on to my lunch while I was running, and Julius had left a lot of comic books up there. He likes the ones with robots, too.

Julius kicked me out of the tree house when he got home. He rides his bike to school. He did say there were a few people missing from my class when roll was called, me being one of them.

So this morning I rode *my* bike to school. And no, I don't have a signed excuse from my mom. She doesn't believe me, about the bus.

You don't believe me either? You think I'm making this up?

Okay, here's a question for you. Where are the Martins? There ought to be three of them in school this year. I asked around and none of them showed up.

Are you absolutely positive they moved away? I mean, their stop is the one before mine, or it always has been. If the Martins were moving, Carrie Martin would have told me. She tells me everything even when I don't want to hear it. And when I was at the mall last week with my mom shopping for clothes I saw Carrie buying red shoes with silver laces. She said she was going to wear them the first day of school.

Carrie doesn't understand color the way I do. She wouldn't know a banana yellow from a lemon yellow. She's nice, she just doesn't quite get it.

Or maybe I should say she *didn't* quite get it.

Go ahead. Call the Martins. I wish you would.

*A few years ago Jane Yolen began spending
about half her time in Scotland. So it's not
surprising that some of her stories, such as this
thrilling sea yarn, are taking on a Scottish flavor.*

SEA DRAGON OF FIFE

Jane Yolen

We found the monster near McBridey's well
on Sunday, after the long kirk service where
Reverend Dougal preached against the dangers
of the sea. He preaches that one at least twice
a year, and most parishioners never tire of it.

The monster wasn't much as monsters go. A
couple of horns, a snubbed snout, nine stubby
talons—one was missing, probably torn off in
a fight—and a tail with three barbs, all quite
worn. But as it was the only monster discovered in Fife this spring, we had to take him.

He died early Monday morning, not from his
wounds but from the lack of a blood meal. We
tracked him to his lair by the trail of ichor, but
did not dare go in. We just waited him out,

knowing that a hungry monster goes quite quickly. One minute snarling and swearing in his monster tongue, and the next minute dead. It's never pretty, but it's lucky for us; otherwise, we'd be overrun with monsters. When we heard the thud in his cave, we waited another hour, then McBridey himself crawled in and stuck a good stout Anster hook in the beast. We towed him out to sea, trawling for a certain sea dragon.

It was Angus McLeod's wife, Annie, who baited the lines for us, sitting on the stone stairs in front of their house and smoking her clay pipe. A braw woman, that, not a bit afraid of any land monster, though even dead it was quite a fright. Most of the women in the cities would have run screaming from it. But Annie was a fisherman's wife and had seen a lot in her life. Besides, she'd just that spring lost her two oldest sons to a great sea dragon, one of the ferocious deep-sea meat-eaters. They'd been plucked off their father's Zulu in front of his disbelieving eyes. Annie was not about to lose Robert, her twelve-year-old, who was next off to sea. She wanted that dragon caught and cooked. So she baited the dragon hook with as much ease as she baited the small lines with mussels for her husband's boat. Not a blink out of her, not over the monster's horns or snout or talons or barbed tail. All the while the smoke from the pipe curled about her head like a halo.

"Done," Annie said, standing and stretching. Like all the McLeods, she was never one for excess conversation.

We loaded the bait monster into McLeod's own Zulu, and the little boat wallowed a bit under the weight, but it was no heavier than a load of haddock, I suppose. And then we were off, the red sails floating nicely on a flanny wind, with its soft and unexpected breezes. Annie waved to us from shore, her other hand tight on young Robert. He was pulling away from her a bit. Twelve is big enough for a man, but she was not about to let him go till that dragon was gone.

It was a mackerel sky, so we didn't need much sail. Still, a Zulu's red sail can look like a banner, and so we flew it to signal that dragon we were coming, like the old clan banners the Highland men hoisted when they went off to fight at Sterling and at Bannockburn. Lord, we were sure of ourselves. Besides, we'd our guns with us, and a couple of harpoons as well. And a big barrel of gunpowder. We would not be taken, like McLeod's two boys, without a fight.

But we came home early, the bait taken— snubbed snout, nine talons, and all. And not so much as a dragon's claw to show for it. We never even saw the beast.

McLeod was in a foul mood, for the dragon had not only gotten the bait but a bit of his red sail as well. He was as "thrawn as a wulf," so his wife put it when we landed, contrary and angry and not to be fooled with. He went off to the pub and did not come home until the wee hours of the morning.

Annie knew better than to wait up for him. But she should have stayed awake on account of Robert. That boy had been growing in leg and thigh and heart since his brothers' deaths, and he would not be treated like a bairn, a child, anymore. He had made up his mind. He was stubborn, like all the McLeods.

When the old man came home from the pub past midnight, his Zulu was gone. And gone, too, was young Robert.

Annie was weeping at the shore in the moonlight, crying, "Robert, Robert . . ." and even "Robin . . ." the bairn's name she had had for him. Her skirt was kilted up and soaking wet, for she had been in the sea after him. But he had never looked back, not even to wave. He did not dare. He was afraid if he saw her crying and calling for him, it would unman him, or so he said later.

He had gone without bait, except for his own

51

self, and with no help at the oars but the good Lord above. But he'd gone to get that brother-killing dragon or die.

McLeod tried to bring Annie inside, but she continued to weep on the shore till all of Anster was awake. And then didn't all the women weep with her, but there was not a one of them in Anster who didn't count the boy gone for good.

"If he is lucky," McAllister said, "drowned first." He didn't say "And eaten after," but we all thought it.

At first light we went out in three swift Fifies to look for him, but no trace of boy or boat did we find. So we had to return home to mourn him like his brothers, with McLeod and his Annie weeping in each other's arms on the pier. A weeping man is a sore sight indeed. But we were too soon with our burial, though we didn't know it then. And what we heard from Robert after was a story indeed.

Robert had sailed north and then west till the wind dropped like a gannet into the water. He just sat there in the Zulu, becalmed, with nothing to do except to think. He was remembering his older brothers, Jamie and Matthew, who had been his idols, the two of them as alike as twins though a year or more apart. They both had had sweethearts in Anster, fisher lassies, who had not taken their loss with any ease, but still came to the cottage and sat with his mother and talked of Jamie and Matthew as if the boys were somehow still alive.

It did not occur to Robert as he sat in the dark on the ocean that he, too, would most likely die there in the dragon's great maw. Lads that age have no fear in them, even fisher lads who have the sea in their bones. He rowed a bit, then rested, then rowed a bit more.

When the sun came up, he was far from sight of land. The sky was first red, then blue above him, the water black below. Robert had been out on the water from the time he had been a babe in arms, but never this far out on his own. Still, he trusted his own skills and his father's little Zulu, it being sturdy and competent like himself. The sun had warmed him by then, so he took off his oilskin, for his jersey was coat enough. And it was that small thing that saved him. The Lord's ways, as Reverend Dougal likes to say, are as unfathomable as the deepest part of the sea.

No sooner had Robert shrugged off his coat and set it on a hook on the mast than a snakey green head and neck, as tall as the mast itself, lifted out of the sea and ripped the oilskin from its resting place. Used to men in their coats being a soft prey, the dragon had mistaken skin for man. Its great hinged jaws—fringed with rows of teeth—opened and closed on the slick coat and carried it triumphantly back into the sea.

Now Robert was a quick lad, though no quicker than Matthew or Jamie, just luckier. And as soon as he had gotten over his startle, he grabbed up the threaded gaffing hook and leaped over the side of the boat after the beast. Though he had never been a horse rider, knowing only the mares of the sea—those great waves that break on the East Neuk shore—he landed astride the sea dragon's neck and knew enough to hold tight with his thighs and grab round with his arms. The sea dragon's scales were as cold and as slippery with foam as a fish's, and the edges of each scale sharp as a honed knife. In the sun the dragon glowed with iridescence, like a hundred sharpened rainbows under him.

Robert had but a moment to be frightened at what he had just done. And a moment to realize that his legs and palms were being slivered. Then he remembered his brothers, whose bodies had never been found.

"You great lump of putresence!" he cried. "You murthering, heathenish fish!" It was a long speech for a McLeod. Paying no attention to his own wounds, he reared back, holding on to the neck with his legs and one hand, and set the hook with all his might into the monster's glistening eye.

The pain of that must have been something horrendous, for the dragon screamed, a sound so loud it was heard all the way to Arbroath, where the fishermen mistook it for a foghorn though the day was fully clear of the haar, the sea mist.

The dragon tossed its head back and forth, its scales now a-glitter with green blood as well as foam. Robert was flung off on the third toss, but luck held him again in its fist, and he landed against the Zulu's bow. Climbing back into the boat, he realized he still had the rope end of the hook in his hand. This he made fast three times around the mast, then tied it with his father's best knot. Then he sank down, exhausted and bleeding from a hundred small cuts that stung with each drop of salt water on them.

But there was no time to rest or to tend his wounds. In its agony the sea dragon had headed down to its watery lair. And if it had gone all the way, that would have been the end—of Zulu and Robert, both. But the hook—luck three times—had caught up under the monster's eyebone, and the pain when the rope had pulled tight was so great, the dragon gave up its dive and turned back to the water's surface, where it fell onto the flat of the sea. There it began to swim, paddling east awkwardly—for it was a deep-sea creature—into the east end of the firth, tail and flippers lashing the water into a froth that bubbled onto the beaches as

far as Queensferry and upsetting a bevy of plea-
sure boats out for the day.

Of course it dragged the little Zulu behind,
with the exhausted Robert hanging on to the
gunnels in terror. But there was nothing he
could do except pray. The morning and afternoon had sped by and night was coming on,
and the dragon kept swimming, towing the
boat and Robert in its wake.

They passed the Isle of May after dark, star-
tling puffins off their nests, then three times
around Bass Rock, and all the while that dragon
tried to rid itself of its unwanted cargo. Then it
headed back west again and out to the open sea.

That hook, made of cold iron, held fast in
the fey creature's head. The Zulu, being of good
East Neuk make, did not break up. And Robert,
like a true Scot, went from terror to anger to
cool courage. His wounds stopped bleeding and
scabbed over; his heart scabbed over, too. He
became a man on that first night, and something even greater by dawn.

He was to say, later, that there had been porpoises on either side of his boat, encouraging
him, some riding ahead like beacons and some
skirling in his wake. But that sounds like fancy
to me, though the storymakers have picked it
up as part of the way they now tell the tale.
Still—how could he have seen porpoises in the
dark? I suspect they were only the haverings

of a hungry, wounded lad, for he had not had a bit of food or drink with him but only some Fisherman's Friend drops he carried for a sore throat. They were all that had sustained him on that wild three-day ride.

Nothing, however, sustained the sea dragon. It ran out of steam by noon of the second day, tried once to stove the little Zulu in, and only succeeded in toppling the already-loosened mast. The mast crashed into the sea where the dragon was lying on its side, exhausted, its ruined eye staring blindly up into the brilliant, cloudless blue sky. Mast hit hook and hammered it with one blow straight into the beast's brain. And there the sea dragon died, a hundred nautical miles from land.

By the time Robert had rowed the little boat home, towing the great carcass behind him, it was a day and a half later. A truly impressive feat. He was aided by some good winds and a fair tide. But he had no mast and no sail to take full advantage. It was desperate work. Only about half the creature remained intact; the sea has its own jackals.

The entire town—all who had turned out for his funeral just two days before and more— came out to greet him in their boats. He was a rare hero, the best of Anster, the best of the entire East Neuk.

When Robert finally reached land, his father

grabbed his hand and held it, tears running down the old man's face. His mother took him by the shoulders and shook him until they were both red in the face. And then she saw the scabs on his palms, and pulling up the legs of his trousers, saw the scabs on his legs. At that, she threw her arms around him and hugged him until they were both breathless and worn. But none of them said a word the whole time. The McLeods were not much for conversation.

Reverend Dougal used that ride as the topic for a month of sermons, each one longer than the last. No one slept a wink at the kirk services, for fear of missing a word of the story.

And what was left of the beast, Annie McLeod salted down. It filled seventeen full barrels and one neat little firkin. Sea dragon tastes a bit like herring cooked on an open fire, only a bit sharper. It was so much in demand, she traded most of the barrels for tatties and neaps, enough to keep the McLeods full and hearty for years to come.

As for young Robert, after that ride, he'd enough of the sea to last him a lifetime. He apprenticed to a blacksmith in St. Andrews and made hooks. Lots of hooks. All of good cold iron.

I understand they are quite the best in all of Britain for killing monsters, on land or under the sea.

We're proud to introduce a new character who we think is going to have an exciting future: George Pinkerton, a full-time librarian who also happens to be a world-class monster-hunter!

GEORGE PINKERTON AND THE BLOODSUCKING FIEND OF BROKENTREE SWAMP

Lawrence Watt-Evans

I had been hanging around the Springfield Library all afternoon. I hadn't found any new books about monsters, but I didn't have anywhere better to go. I was about to head home when the phone rang.

Mrs. Garcia answered it, and I sort of tried to listen, not really snooping, just standing around nearby. I couldn't hear much, though—whoever was on the other end wasn't very loud.

Then Mrs. Garcia covered the mouthpiece with her hand and looked around and of course she saw me, since I was standing right there. "Billy, have you seen Mr. Pinkerton?"

"Sure. He's in the stacks." (That's what they call the shelves where they keep all the books, the stacks.)

Mrs. Garcia uncovered the phone. "If you could hold on a moment I'll see if I can find him." She put the phone on the desk and headed for the other side of the library.

I looked at that phone for a minute. Someone must be calling about a case, I thought. Mr. Pinkerton doesn't have a wife or kids or anything, and he hardly ever gets personal calls at work. If it was a case, that meant he was going to go off fighting monsters again. If I worked things right I might be able to go with him.

At least, if he was talked into taking the case. If the monsters aren't hurting anyone, he won't touch them. He always says he'd rather read about monsters than meet them, same as he'd rather read about a war than fight in one. He never planned to get into the monster business; he was just good at it.

It all started when a maniac turned a bunch of zombies loose here in Springfield, Indiana, and no one but Mr. Pinkerton was able to stop them. That was how we met. I was in the library at the time, and he needed a hand with some details, so I helped out a little—but just a little. Mr. Pinkerton did all the dangerous stuff. He doesn't lift weights or have a handsome face or anything, but he was a real hero—he saved the town.

61

A couple of months later my brother, who's in the navy, told me they were having trouble with a giant squid, and I suggested he talk to Mr. Pinkerton. Next thing I knew the navy had hired Mr. Pinkerton as a consultant. Since then a lot of people have called him about monsters, and when I'm lucky I've managed to tag along and help out.

Not that I wanted anyone to get hurt or anything, but I sort of hoped that monsters were causing real trouble somewhere. So I picked up the phone, which I probably shouldn't have, but no one had actually told me *not* to.

"I'm Billy Barnett," I said in my deepest, most mature voice. "I'm Mr. Pinkerton's associate. Could you tell me a little about your situation, please?"

"My name's Aloysius Brown," the voice on the other end said. He had a Southern accent, like the country singers on TV. "I'm the sheriff of Brokentree County, Tennessee. Seems we might have a vampire loose here, and we'd like your Mr. Pinkerton to come take a look."

"A vampire?" I said. "I wouldn't think that would be all that difficult to deal with, once you know it's a vampire." After all, everybody knew about vampires from the movies—you keep them away with crosses and garlic, and kill them with stakes through the heart.

"I wouldn't have thought so, either—not that

I gave much thought to vampires before this week—but this one's giving us plenty of trouble. The state police and the FBI don't know a thing about vampires, and I saw a newspaper piece about Mr. Pinkerton's work for the navy, so I thought he might be able to help. I sure hope so—we've got two good people dead so far."

That scared me a little. If people were getting killed, this was serious. But it meant that Mr. Pinkerton would take it seriously, too.

"Sheriff," I said, "Mr. Pinkerton should be here in a minute, and you can tell him all about it. First, let me explain a few things about how Mr. Pinkerton works. If he does decide to go down to Tennessee, we'll need two seats on the first available flight. We might need to send a few things by air express freight as well. You'll be expected to cover all our expenses, and pay an additional fee. . . ."

That was as far as I'd gotten when I heard voices. "Here comes Mr. Pinkerton now," I said quickly, and put the phone down.

I was pretty sure Mr. Pinkerton had seen this—he doesn't miss much. But he just picked up the phone. "This is George Pinkerton."

For a minute he listened. Then he said, "I'm just a librarian. Yes, I know a lot about monsters, because I've studied them in books, but anyone could. If this is an ordinary vampire . . ."

63

Then he stopped, and frowned.

"Two people killed?" he said. "Both exsanguinated?"

"Both what?" I asked.

He covered the mouthpiece. "Exsanguinated. It means 'drained of blood.' "

I marveled at that—who'd think there would be a word for it?

"You've searched for a coffin?" Mr. Pinkerton asked. "It wouldn't necessarily look like a traditional coffin, you know—any big box . . ."

Sheriff Brown must have interrupted him, because Mr. Pinkerton didn't finish the sentence. A moment later he sighed.

"I don't promise I can do anything," he said, "but I'll try. Tell me how to get there." He fished a pen and a piece of scrap paper off the desk.

He listened some more, took notes, then suddenly threw me a look through his thick glasses, tightening his lips so his beard bristled. I sort of grinned back, pretending it was nothing. He settled a few more details with Sheriff Brown, then hung up the phone and glared at me.

"My *associate*, huh?"

I nodded.

He glared a moment longer, then threw up his hands. "Oh, why not? If it's okay with your family, you can come."

*   *   *

Early the next morning we boarded a plane to Knoxville, and Mr. Pinkerton filled me in on the case. The first murder had been a Mrs. McGillicuddy. The sheriff said that on hot nights she slept out on her back porch, to save on air-conditioning. One morning that week her sister had discovered her there—dead. They'd called in a doctor from Oak Ridge, a bigger town a few miles away. She took a good look at the body, then announced that there wasn't a drop of blood left in the woman's veins.

Everyone in town knew what that meant. Sure, a few folks said it was all nonsense, that there wasn't any such thing as a vampire, but most people didn't want to take any chances. The sheriff said that once word got out the K-mart down the road in Brileysburg sold out their entire stock of crosses in just two hours. The local supermarket sold out of garlic by suppertime, and some of the nearby jewelers spent the whole day melting down silver to make bullets and more crosses. Just in case, a few people in town had even added Stars of David, or Islamic crescent-and-star emblems, or other religious insignia. And Father Genetti, the priest in Brileysburg, had even let some people fill squirt guns with holy water.

It hadn't done any good. Two nights later old Mr. Densmore was killed—all the blood sucked out through a hole in his neck. And

Mr. Densmore had had a bunch of garlic, a cross, and a Star of David on each window, a squirt gun of holy water at his bedside, and another cross around his neck. The vampire, if it was a vampire that killed him, had apparently smashed right through one of the windows. The crosses and garlic didn't seem to have bothered it a bit.

The sheriff and his deputies had looked everywhere for any sign of the killer, without success. One deputy thought he'd seen a faint trail from Mr. Densmore's house down to the swamp, but he wasn't sure, and no one could find a single footprint.

A vampire was bad enough. A vampire like this one that wasn't stopped by the usual methods was really awful. Everyone was terrified.

Sheriff Brown had organized a posse to search every attic and basement in town, looking for the vampire's coffin, but hadn't found anything—no coffin, no oversized trunks, no big wooden crates, nothing. He'd just about run out of ideas by the time he phoned the Springfield Library.

We landed in Knoxville and rented a car. Mr. Pinkerton picked up the box of supplies he'd checked as luggage, and loaded everything in the trunk. "It's not far from here, Billy," he said. We drove past Oak Ridge, where the government does a lot of research on nuclear stuff, through Brileysburg, to Brokentree.

I don't know whether the sheriff had made some sort of announcement or what, but word had definitely gotten around. When we rolled into the town—which consisted of maybe three blocks in each direction and then just woods and hills and swamp—a crowd that looked like the entire population of Brokentree, Tennessee, was watching.

We stopped in front of a little wooden building with a flag and a sign out front saying U.S. POST OFFICE. I watched the crowd's faces as Mr. Pinkerton got out of the car. Some of them looked kind of surprised. Mr. Pinkerton's just average height, with narrow shoulders and a bit of a potbelly. A beard and thick glasses hide most of his face, and he was wearing a baggy striped shirt and old jeans. He's not the heroic figure you'd expect a monster hunter to be.

"Mr. Pinkerton?" said a man in a brown uniform and a Smokey the Bear hat. He stepped forward from the crowd and held out a hand. "I'm Aloysius Brown."

"Pleased to meet you," Mr. Pinkerton said as he shook the sheriff's hand.

"And I'm Billy Barnett," I said.

The sheriff shook my hand, too, but he looked at me a bit funny.

"You sounded older on the phone," he said, which I guess was his way of being polite.

"I tried to," I said.

He didn't say any more about it. Instead he just told us, "If you'd like to come to my office, we can discuss the case."

Mr. Pinkerton hesitated, and looked around at the town. "There's something else I'd like to do first, Sheriff. Right away, in fact."

"What would that be?"

"I'll explain in a moment," Mr. Pinkerton said. "Now, you think you have a vampire loose around here?"

"That's what it looks like. The doctor can tell you—"

Mr. Pinkerton held up a hand. "We'll start with this idea of mine first, if you don't mind; then maybe I'll talk to your doctor."

The sheriff frowned. "What idea?"

"Well, unless there are more houses tucked away somewhere I can't see, I'd say Brokentree is a very small town. Perhaps a hundred people?"

"Ninety-two," the sheriff said. "It was ninety-four a week ago."

"So you'd notice a stranger. When I drove in you seemed quite sure who I was."

The sheriff nodded.

"Well, maybe you've already thought of this, but if you do have a vampire here, chances are

68

it's one of your ninety-two people. You'd notice a stranger."

Sheriff Brown blinked. "Well, I'd thought something along those lines. . . ."

Mr. Pinkerton waved his hand at the cloudless blue sky and the bright sun. "Traditional vampires don't come out in open sunlight. It looks to me as if you have just about the entire town standing around right now. You can count your people and see who's missing. If everyone's here, then at least you know that it wasn't one of your own who became a vampire."

"Good point," Sheriff Brown agreed. He turned, raised his arms, and called out, "All right, everyone, line up! Let's see if we're all here!"

A few minutes later he'd run down the line and counted ninety-one people, including himself.

"Where's Tom Adams?" asked a boy my age.

For a moment everyone looked back and forth.

"He must be the vampire!" a woman shouted.

"Oh, don't be silly," another woman protested. "He just didn't know Mr. Pinkerton was coming!"

"Who's Tom Adams?" Mr. Pinkerton asked.

"You might say he's the town hermit," the sheriff explained. "He lives by himself in a cabin down by the swamp."

Mr. Pinkerton nodded thoughtfully. "And where were the two killings?"

The sheriff pointed. "Mrs. McGillicuddy lived in the last house on Willow Street, and Harvey Densmore's place is there at the bend in Water Street." He noticed Mr. Pinkerton's inquiring expression, and explained, "We've got three streets running east and west—Main here in the middle, First Street to the north, and Water Street alongside the swamp to the south, running down to the river. The cross streets are all named for trees—Willow's at the foot of the hill."

"And this Tom Adams . . ."

"His place is back off Water Street a few hundred yards."

"And Mrs. McGillicuddy lived at the corner of Water and Willow?"

"More or less," the sheriff agreed.

"Well, I must admit this Tom Adams is a likely candidate. Let's go have a word with him.'"

A few minutes later Sheriff Brown knocked on the door of Tom Adams' cabin, while Mr. Pinkerton and I stood by, watching. They had convinced the rest of the town to stay back; there wasn't any point in confronting a suspect with a mob.

No one answered the sheriff's knock, not

even when he pounded heavily on the door with his fist.

At last he stepped back and charged at the door with his shoulder. Just like on TV. The latch snapped, and the door burst in.

I hurried in, before anyone could stop me. But then I sort of wished I hadn't, because it meant I was the first to see what was left of Tom Adams. I made a noise, sort of a gasp.

Tom Adams wasn't the vampire. Tom Adams was the third victim. His throat was all torn open—the holes weren't neat little spots like in the movies; they were great big red openings. They looked horrible.

I turned away so I wouldn't be sick. Mr. Pinkerton studied the area around the dead man—the bed and the smashed window in the cabin's rear wall and the floor. He pointed to the braided rug on the floor, and then the rumpled blanket on the bed. "They're wet," he said.

"Well, the swamp's right out back," the sheriff said. "Whoever did this probably waded through it to hide his trail."

Mr. Pinkerton frowned. "Your traditional vampire doesn't need to hide his trail."

"Maybe it's not a vampire at all," the sheriff said. "Maybe it's just some crazy person." He shuddered. "They'd have to be crazy, to wade through the swamp!"

"Oh?" Mr. Pinkerton said. "Why?"

"It's full of snakes and leeches and bugs," the sheriff said. "Used to be gators, too, though nobody's seen any lately."

Mr. Pinkerton nodded thoughtfully. "Perhaps we could go back to my car," he said.

The sheriff nodded. "I need to get the doctor. And if whoever did this went through the swamp we won't be able to track him, anyway."

We all hiked back up to Main Street. Sheriff Brown went to his office, and Mr. Pinkerton and I headed for the car. A bunch of people were still hanging around the post office and watched curiously as Mr. Pinkerton opened the trunk. If they were expecting high-tech monster-hunting gear, that wasn't what they got.

What they got was books.

The entire trunk was full of them, hundreds of books—old, new, big, little, hardcovers and paperbacks. As Mr. Pinkerton always said, he was a librarian—everything he knew came from books, and when he traveled on monster business he brought along his own personal monster library.

He selected an armful. He handed me an old book about Tennessee folklore and said, "See what you can find."

Then we sat side by side on the sidewalk, looking for anything that might help, until

Sheriff Brown came out of his office. Mr. Pinkerton looked up from a big black book.

"We've been doing a little research," he explained. "We are clearly not dealing with the traditional western vampire, since they can't pass the cross or tolerate garlic, nor do they leave a trail, or need to break in a window to get through it."

"Maybe the vampire heaved a rock through the window to knock the stuff out of the way," I suggested.

Mr. Pinkerton shook his head. "No, I'm afraid that simply isn't the way vampires work. Tom Adams was wearing a cross around his neck, in any case." He put down his book and picked up another from the pile beside him. "Now, the Chinese vampire, or *kiang-shi*, is violent and brutal, and would not be stopped by crosses, but cannot abide the smell of garlic. I think we can eliminate that possibility. The Australian *yara-ma-yha-who* never enters homes, but only attacks travelers. The Ashanti *obayifo*, from Africa, and the Malaysian and Filipino vampires prey primarily on children rather than adults." He slammed the book shut and set it on top of the others.

"What we are dealing with," he said, "is not any documented variety of vampire."

"I can't find any local legends that fit, either," I said, putting down my own book.

"There aren't any stories about bloodsucking monsters in Tennessee. So if it's not a vampire, what could it be? What else sucks blood?"

"The sheriff told us that, Billy," Mr. Pinkerton replied. "Think about it. Sheriff, I would say that in this case, crosses and garlic and stakes through the heart are not what we need. Do you have a shotgun I could borrow?"

Sheriff Brown blinked in surprise. "A shotgun?"

"And buckshot," Mr. Pinkerton said.

"*I* told you something?" the sheriff asked, puzzled.

"Indeed you did," Mr. Pinkerton said, getting to his feet and dumping the stack of books back into the trunk of his car. "You told me exactly what I needed to be reminded of. I'd be glad of your company, Sheriff—I'd like to do a little hunting."

The sheriff looked at me, but I just shrugged. "You're the expert, Mr. Pinkerton," he said.

Twenty minutes later I kept a lookout from the edge of Brokentree Swamp as the sheriff and Mr. Pinkerton slogged through the swamp in waders that went up to their waists. Each of them carried a twelve-gauge pump-action shotgun over the black water. When they had gone out about sixty feet, they turned and started wading parallel to the shore. I followed

along the soggy ground, staying as close as I could.

I thought I saw something in the muck beyond them. I squinted, trying to make out what it was—maybe there were still gators out there after all. It didn't look like one, though. It just looked like a big black shadow under the water—an old log, maybe, about ten feet long.

"What are we hunting, Mr. Pinkerton?" the sheriff asked, echoing my thoughts as he squinted into the gloom under the thick, vine-covered trees. "I'd think you were after gators, but they don't suck anyone's blood, and no one's seen any lately." He poked at some weeds with the barrel of his shotgun.

That shadow almost seemed to be following Mr. Pinkerton, I thought. Then I realized that it probably *was* his shadow, so of course it was following him.

"The gators gave me a clue, but they aren't what we're after," Mr. Pinkerton said. "I think you'll see soon, and if I told you, you wouldn't . . ."

Wait, there *was* something in the water—I was sure of it! All of a sudden I knew it couldn't be Mr. Pinkerton's shadow because it was on the wrong side, the side toward the sun. Whatever it was, it was big, and it had picked up speed, and it was moving straight toward them!

76

"Behind you!" I shrieked, and ran into the murky water, and never mind that I didn't have any waders.

The two of them turned toward me. "Billy, get back!" Mr. Pinkerton shouted.

"Behind you!" I shouted again. As I pointed, and splashed up and down, a huge humped shape started to heave itself up from the water. I watched in terror as that thing reared up and up and up . . . it must have stood eight feet out of the water with more underneath that I couldn't see supporting it as it swung upright. It was a hideous shiny black thing, reaching a horrible gripping mouth for Mr. Pinkerton's throat. Except for some stubby, crooked little legs waving in the air I couldn't make out eyes or much of anything else except for that *mouth.*

I yelled and yelled, and it seemed as if Mr. Pinkerton and the sheriff just kept staring at me rather than where I was pointing. It couldn't have been more than a second or two, but it seemed like forever before they finally turned the rest of the way around and saw the thing. Then Mr. Pinkerton was face to face with it. Just in time he dove sideways, splashing into the swamp. The thing loomed forward.

The sheriff acted fast—his shotgun roared, and with a sickening thud the creature instantly exploded, splattering the swamp and everything in its path with more blood than I had ever imagined anything could hold. The water turned a bright ugly red for a dozen feet in every direction. Mr. Pinkerton stood up again.

Ignoring the blood, the sheriff sloshed forward and pumped two more shots into the oozing black mess, just to be certain it was really dead. Then he stood, panting. As the echoes of the shotgun blasts faded in the trees, he stared down at what was left of the creature.

"What was that thing?" he asked, his voice trembling.

"A leech," said Mr. Pinkerton, wiping dripping hair off his face. "A giant mutant leech—as I suspected." He coughed. "When you and Billy asked what else sucked blood, and you mentioned leeches in the swamp, I put two and two together. Something must have drastically altered its genetic composition, made it grow into a monster." He shuddered. "Could it have been radiation from the experiments over at Oak Ridge? At any rate, it was a *hungry* giant mutant leech. I'd guess as it grew bigger it preyed on the alligators, until it had killed them all off. When there wasn't anything left in the swamp big enough to feed it, it went ashore to hunt."

Mr. Pinkerton turned toward me. "Thanks

for the warning, Billy. I would have been its next meal."

"Glad to be of help, Mr. Pinkerton," I answered shakily.

"A leech," murmured the sheriff as he stared at the dead monster. Now that it was dead, he looked like he was going to be sick. By then he probably wished it *were* a vampire.

I'd come across leeches in swimming holes before. They're nasty slimy black bloodsuckers that can stick onto you. Normally they're only an inch or two long. I'd thought those were bad, but now I thought about a leech ten feet long, and smart enough to come ashore for food. I looked at the blood and gore congealing in a layer on the surface of the swamp. "Eeeeew," I said to myself.

Mr. Pinkerton found a handkerchief inside a pocket and wiped some of the blood and swamp goo from his glasses. "You'll want to keep an eye out in case there are any more, but I'd say we've solved your problem." He straightened up and tugged at his shirt, trying to look businesslike even though he was standing in the middle of a swamp with blood and muck dripping thickly through his beard. "Now," he said, "about my fee . . ."

When Lawrence Schimel heard we were doing another monster book, he used it as an excuse to cook up some mischief. . . .

A RECIPE FOR TROUBLE

Lawrence Schimel

Ingredients:

1 hot summer evening
1 full moon
1–2 Monsters Under the Bed
1–2 Monsters in the Closet
2–3 kids, trying to fall asleep

Directions:

1. Preheat the evening with a summer afternoon, sun shining down so strong it melts the asphalt.

2. Place the kids on a bed of lettuce, rays of moonlight streaming in through the window to keep them awake.

3. In a small bowl to one side, stir the monsters slowly. Scrape the sides of the bowl with the spoon loudly enough for the kids to hear.

4. When the kids have risen from their fear, poke them down again and turn out onto a floor dusted with flour. This will leave a trail for the monsters to follow.

5. Drain their courage, and let the kids simmer in a covered pot. Each minute you wait will seem like an hour to them.

6. Toss in the monsters and whisk vigorously.

7. Lock the door and throw away the key.

You now have plenty of trouble to go around. Serves 2–4 monsters, depending on how hungry they are.

When I was a kid one of my favorite things in the world was the Spook House at the amusement park. But much as I loved it, I always wanted the monsters to be even better than they were.
On the other hand, I'm not sure I wanted them to be quite this good. . . .

THE SPOOK MAN

Al Sarrantonio

The Spook Man came to town.

Mothers and fathers locked their doors. Dogs hid in doghouses. Mailmen, ignoring their credo, left mail undelivered and went to bars or home to scolding wives. Schools closed up, locked and bolted their playground gates and sealed their windows. The grasses turned brown; even the weather changed, trading warmth for sudden chill and seeping sunshine for blustery blocks of gray-black clouds. The town tried to hide.

The Spook Man set up on the edge of a baseball field. His rolling home was a brooding many-wheeled thing in All-Souls' colors; those that chanced to look at it said it was as big as a house or as small as a horse-trailer. No two gave the same description. Some said it had a hundred windows, hung with black lace and with flowerpots filled with dead daisies; others described it as sad and shallow, a hobo's retreat. There were gables and then there weren't. A turret and then not. A porch with a jet-black rocking chair that vanished into thin air. A steeple that became nothing. Soon no one looked at it.

The waiting began. Children were locked in cellars, kept in tight bedrooms, told to glue themselves, literally, to television sets. Children were overfed, told to eat and keep their eyes off the windows. Most boarded up their windows, sealed them tight against the dim brown light that suffused everything and tried to leak in. Telephone games became the rule of the day: Susie called Billie called Carl called Maisie. Parents kept a watchful ear to see that games and TV were all that were talked about. Parents were everywhere children were; there was more parent-love exhibited than ever before, and this made Susie and Billie and Pete and Jerry and all the rest nervous.

The Spook Man waited.

Four houses kept four children locked up especially tight. These were Harry and Brenda and Chubby and Larry—the four who lived, breathed, and ate monsters. When the new werewolf movie came out they were first on line; when the binding wire was snipped from the new eerie comics, they were hovering there with greedy eyes. No plastic creature model escaped them; no fright mask wasn't in their possession. Wax fangs covered their cavities; they walked in shuffling limps; spoke in Igor voices or baying howls.

Harry and Brenda and Chubby and Larry plotted. Each in their own house, with parents floating like balloons nearby, they used their Code.

"I love the TV I saw last night," Harry told Brenda.

"We'll meet tonight to see the Spook Man," is what he meant.

"I ate a dozen cookies at one sitting yesterday," Chubby told Larry.

"Tonight the Spook Man," is what he said.

"Good books to read," is what Harry told them all.

"Ten-thirty by the playground gate," is what they knew.

As obedient as ever, the four watched television, read books and played games. They smiled like they always did. Then bedtime came, and the light went off, and each in turn climbed carefully out of pried-open windows.

They arrived in concert as a half-moon broke

through the low sky. The clouds scudded, making the moon blink, and as it shone again, their eyes turned like pin-magnets on the Spook Man's place.

It was a house. This was no hobo's retreat. It was a house as sure as any of them lived in one. There were windows and a steeple and gables and a porch, and there was that jet-black rocking chair. It was magnificent and frightening. Victorian, Georgian, Tudor. Massive.

Bleak.

"Where are the wheels, how did it get there?" asked Chubby.

"I don't want to be here," said Larry.

"Come on," said Harry and Brenda at the same time.

There was only one door, a dark one of metal, and they crept up to it. The sky overhead played tricks, turned bright and dark and all the colors of a thunderstorm. A thunderstorm threatened, went away, came back. Went away.

They reached the door.

The door opened.

The Spook Man was there.

"Ah," he said, from somewhere beneath his cape. The cape fluttered, twirled, snapped. A face was revealed, quickly hidden. Powder-white, red-tinted, empty, sharp. Behind him a thousand fireflies seemed to hover, blinking Christmas tree colors. There were mirrors back there, and curtains, and strings of hanging beads that tinkled in the swirling bellows breeze. And other things lurking.

"Come into my ghost cellar," the Spook Man whispered to Harry and Brenda and Larry and Chubby. His breath was apple wine, blossoms on a chill wind, October.

"Come in and see what's here," the Spook Man breathed at them. "Come see my ghosts and ghoulies. I have things that bump in the night and all day long. I have men with rubber faces. I have orange and black bats, and a hag with fingernails ten inches long. I have cats galore, with eyes so bright green and teeth so sharp you'll shudder. I have skeletons of white bone marble, bones that clack one against the other like graveside cymbals. There are red crisp Halloween apples with fangmarks in them, dunked for by vampires. The vampires are there too, red and black and hidden in upper corners with the spiders. There is something that looks like Jell-O that oozes when you speak to it; something else so horrible that I've left it unnamed. *You* can name it," he said, pointing one long and insubstantial finger into Chubby's jacket-covered belly. "Or you or you or you," he continued, pointing to them all. He pulled his finger back, making a steeple with all of his fingers and leaning down over it to hover, helicopterlike, above them. "Won't you *please* come in?"

"Sure we will," Harry blustered, pushing in front of the rest. He was brown, crisp haired, and bold, leader of the Four. "That's why we're here, isn't it?"

No one challenged him, but no one moved to follow either.

He mounted the short steps, passing under the Spook Man's cape. "Come on," he said.

They did.

"Excellent!" the Spook Man hissed, rolling his cape over each in turn like a bullfighter, counting each upon the head as he passed. He tapped Brenda twice, causing her to look at him from beneath her red hair.

"Twice knocks for red locks," the Spook Man said, smiling a grin that put wonderful goosepimply hands round her heart.

They found themselves in a black hallway, and when they looked back for guidance the Spook Man was gone. A black wall cutting off the outside world was in his place.

"He's just trying to scare us," Harry said, some of the bluster gone from his voice.

"D-doing a good job," said Larry, youngest and least true of the quartet.

"Ahh," was Harry's reply, and they proceeded.

They felt along the walls, and the walls were

damp and slippery. They were crypt walls. They gave off the smell of underground, as underground they went in a gentle slope.

Suddenly, piling one on the other in the darkness, there was a door with a white face on it.

Larry screamed, and Brenda and Chubby and Harry merely shivered.

The face looked through them with the bottomless holes of its eyes.

And said, "Quiet."

It was a Marley face, a face cut from the cloth of ghosts. It shimmered in and out of vision, now sharp, now wavering, now sharp again. It asked them their business. When they didn't answer, it asked who had sent them.

"The Spook Man," Brenda said in a rush.

"The *Spook* Man," the face intoned.

The door melted away, showing a stairway of glowing green steps leading down into absolute black. There could have been a great and deep hole in the earth on either side of those steps, for all they could see. There were steps, and nothing else.

"Let's," Harry said tentatively, meekly, and maybe-we-shouldn'tly, "go."

"No," breathed the other three, but again they followed.

The steps sang like chimes. Soon, as the four of them stepped down, a harplike mix of bells rang out. The tones became deeper as they sank into the darkness, turning by sneaky degrees to the middling screech of a stepped-on cat and then to the deep bellow of a funeral mass organ. The tones grew so low and thundering their stomachs rumbled. They looked back to see that the lights disappeared as they left them behind, and, to their horror, they found that along with the lights the steps disappeared too.

They found themselves at the bottom, huddled together, four bodies in the dark trying to fit into the space of one.

"I'm *scared*," Larry said.

"Don't be," Harry countered.

"Why not?" asked Chubby.

"Don't know," Harry admitted.

"Come on," said Brenda this time.

The darkness drifted before them. They sensed something just out of reach, taunting them, debating whether to move back or strike. Things ticked along the floor, brushed at their legs. Chubby felt a clawed thing grab his ankle and release it in the same movement. Dusty things brushed their faces. When they covered their faces, dusty things brushed their hands.

"I'm *scared!*" Larry repeated.

"You're supposed to be," Harry tried, as all around them it grew lighter.

They could see themselves now, their

trembling arms and deliciously knocking knees. They could see each other's wild faces. With quick eyes they looked down for the crawling, drifting things, but saw nothing.

A door creaked open in front of them.

"I'm scared! I'm scared!" Larry screamed, turning to flee.

Something held him back. There was a wall a foot behind them moving up on them all the time, compelling them to move on. Larry scratched at it, beginning to cry. Harry and Chubby grabbed him, pulled him through the doorway after them.

A voice sounded, the Spook Man's voice, and Larry quieted immediately.

"Welcome to my cellar," it said.

Blackness descended then. And then a cacophony of lights.

Fangs, radium-bright, flew at them from every corner. Deep and ponderous chains were dragged before them, around them. A cauldron made its appearance, bubbling and roiling green-hot liquid. It stirred itself, and then was stirred in turn by the vilest of witches—warts, cackle, and all. The cauldron evaporated, and then the witch was on her broom, coming straight at them and veering up and over at the last second in a steep angle. Skulls appeared at the four corners of the room, at headheight, and then skeletons winked into view below them. A skeletal rattle-dance commenced.

Harry and Chubby and Brenda danced with it. All hints of fear had gone, replaced by wild abandon. They danced like wood creatures, aping the gestures of their bony mates. They laughed.

Larry tried to laugh. Instead he made a compromise, painting his mouth with a horrible rictuslike smile that did little to hide his paralysis. He was paralyzed by fear; horrified by the revel of his wild friends. He wanted to be home, under the sheets and under layer on layer of patchwork quilt, listening to nothing but his own even breathing and the silence of his self-made night. He wanted Mother and Father to be out in the living room, further boarding the windows. He wanted Sis to be in the bedroom next door, sleeping safe with her lemon-yellow duck clasped under her sucking thumb. He wanted the TV to be on; the radio to be on; he wanted to play games, Scrabble and Parcheesi and hearts and rummy. He wanted, along with everyone else, the Spook Man to be gone.

Larry's grin grew wider.

The monsters came now.

Brenda and Harry and Chubby cheered. Here they all were, the models they had built and the comics they had collected come to life.

They came in a dancing procession, out of the dark and back into it again. First Frankenstein, green, square, and parading false life, his arms frozen in front; then Dracula—no, *two* Draculas, snarling and circling each other like caged lady tigers, each seeking to snap redly at the other's neck. Mummies followed; then wolf-men howling at artificial moons that blinked on above; then sea creatures of all sorts, dripping seaweed and smelling of salt and rotting fish. Then the invaders from Space, each more tentacled and more colorful than the one preceding, with breathing apparatus and bulging eyes. There were bat-men and bat-women, giant insects galore, a gaggle of hairless beasts slowly diminishing in number as the gluttonous blob-creature behind them ate them off one at a time. There were men with pumpkin heads and men with fly heads, men with dogs' heads, men with no heads. Growling rabbits. Mammoth frogs. Titanic rats, some so crazed they were eating themselves. Armless, legless, eyeless things; things that crawled and snapped and clicked; slimy things; things that went *flit* and were gone before they could be identified. Creatures of the night. Creatures of every underground imagination.

Horrid things.

Chubby and Brenda and Harry celebrated each monster's passing. With each new fright

their huzzahs grew. Here was every nightmare they had ever dreamed about served up like breakfast, the nastiest breakfast there ever was. The monsters came and went, invoking death and rot and damp earth.

Chubby suddenly stopped cheering.

As if a spell had broken, he looked at the faces of his three friends and found only on Larry's what he wanted to see.

"I don't think this is so much fun anymore," he said in a bare whisper.

Larry looked at him with hope; Harry and Brenda were lost in the procession of evil.

"I think I want to leave," Chubby said a little louder.

"I want to go home," Larry joined in without hesitation.

Harry and Brenda showed no interest in them.

"I don't want to be here!" Larry shouted above the flapping of batwings, the bellowing of the not-alive.

Brenda grabbed him and howled, demonlike, into his face.

Chubby momentarily lost himself again, becoming a wild thing. The three of them danced a witches' ring around Larry, screeching and tearing at their hair. The other monsters were gone. They formed a wider circle, and fairy lights, wisps of pale bright shooting stars, twirled round with them.

The terror burst out of Larry.

"I don't want to be here!" he screamed, "I never meant any of it, never believed any of it! I don't like spiders and toads and snakes—I'm scared of mice! I built monster models, but I built model cars and ships and planes too. I read *Creepy* and *Strange* and *Ghoul* and *Monster* comics but I also read *Archie* and *Superman*. I snuck out to the movies to see Westerns and funny movies, instead of always watching the Wolfman. I threw out the model guillotine you made me build; I like to collect coins and baseball cards, and stamps." He was crying now. *"I don't even like the nighttime—I'm afraid of the dark!"*

The wild dance stopped. Chubby stepped over with Larry, hung his head.

"Me," he muttered, "too."

Brenda and Harry stood, unmoved. There was a wild ruby gleam in their eyes; their faces seemed more elongated, their ears sharper edged.

"We want to go home!" Chubby and Larry begged.

A door opened in the darkness.

It was a rectangle cut out of nothing, leading to the outside night. There was the baseball field, there the chainlink fence they had climbed, a few bare trees all bathed in velvet moonlight.

Larry and Chubby ran through the door.

All around Brenda and Harry there was a booming laugh.

The Spook Man appeared.

His face was less indistinct now, yet still indescribable. He seemed less sinister, more of normal height and painted in daytime colors.

"Two is more than I ever hope for," he said almost gently. He made a cape motion at the two fleeing figures outside, now climbing like quick monkeys over the fence and away. "They won't be scared for long. In time it will be almost a pleasant memory for them, a visit to a funhouse."

He turned that elusive face on Brenda and Harry.

"Which is what this is—a funhouse—if you've the right stomach for it." His voice became both echoes and hushed. "Town to town, and hardly ever more than one. Many times none at all." His eyes, piercing, hooded, seemed to be searching for something in their faces, a beacon. "They really don't know me, all the little people in these little towns. They're afraid of me and my little family. But they don't know."

He leaned down over them, a midnight hawk looming over its brood or prey. "Little red and little black," he continued, looking from Brenda to Harry. "Are you ready to join my family? You saw them, all the goblins and friends and ghosts and demons there are. Once all of them looked just like you, little pink or yellow or ebony people with creature model kits and monster magazines. But something breathed inside them, behind the ghoul costumes and playthings, something locked in the crypts of their human bodies and straining to get out. They loved monsters so much they wanted to *be* monsters. I gave them the chance. I called them—never took them, only called—away from their creature features and werewolf masks and horror novels, and gave them the chance to join their real family. The one that would make their lives complete. Only the true ones stay, of course. Here they breathe with their real lungs and fly with their real wings, cocooning into the beautiful little horrors they want to be."

He leaned even closer, his face becoming the shifting meadow of monstrous shapes, a nightmare triptych mirroring the life he offered. "So, little ones," he said, his voice echoing all around them as his cape flowed out to encircle, hold them fast to his world, "are you ready to become my tiny son, my baby daughter? Do you want to see how much you really love monsters?"

"*No!*"

Harry pushed out at the cape, ducking under its strong black wings and out through the doorway. Soon his feet made the chainlink fence jangle as his sneakers carried him up, over, and gone.

The Spook Man laughed softly. "Hardly ever more than one," he said, half to himself.

He turned slowly back to Brenda.

"And you, little crimson, have *you* made up *your* mind?"

Brenda made no answer.

The Spook Man laughed a booming laugh then, and the doorway to the world zipped shut, and the brothers and sisters of the night came from their caskets and damp niches and dusty tombs to meet their new sibling, the creature of teeth and claws and wild red eyes that danced before them.

*When King Arthur was a boy, his true identity
was kept a secret; only Merlin the Magician
knew what lay in store for him.
Of course, in order for Arthur to grow up and
become king, the first thing he had to do was
survive his childhood—no easy thing, given the
scrapes he and his foster brother Cai were
constantly getting into. Scrapes like the one Cai
tells about here, involving a boy who wants
to be a wizard.*

THE WIZARD OF CHAOS

Michael Markiewicz

We were crossing Tonkin's Bridge, and already
late, but that wasn't our biggest problem.

"It's your fault, Cai!" screamed my younger
brother, Arthur, as he dropped his bundles and
sat defiantly on the railing of the bridge.

"*I'm* not the one who lost the list," I answered firmly.

We had been sent to town by our godfather,
Merlin, and Arthur had forgotten to buy one of
the wizard's magical supplies. Merlin had said

quite specifically, and with his best "I'll turn you into something horrible" voice—"Don't forget the mustard!"

It wasn't that he liked mustard on his meat. Merlin used it for spells . . . and was getting ready for something big. He told us he was having bad dreams, and for a wizard that could be serious.

He'd been in his study for hours the day before. Finally he sent us to town for some things so that he would have time to prepare spells. We were all supposed to go to the annual wizard's council the next day at Callen, and Merlin said he needed to be ready. But now it looked as if he wouldn't be.

Arthur folded his arms and snorted. "I'm not walking all the way back there because you forgot—"

"I didn't forget! I never tried to remember, because you had a list!" I screamed.

"But I lost it."

"So that's your fault," I insisted.

"But you're older. You should have remembered!"

"Well, you shouldn't have lost it!"

"You're just stupid!"

"And you're just more stupid!"

I was so mad I started to leave without him. Unfortunately, I wasn't looking where I was going, and my foot squished into a pile of horse droppings right in the middle of the bridge. A swarm of flies rose off the putrid pile and surrounded my head like a buzzing cloud. Then, as I was trying to scrape the smelly gunk off my boot with a stick, one of the flies went right into my ear. I hated flies.

Arthur started to laugh.

"You're as dumb as a Saxon with half his brains missing!" he giggled.

Now I was really mad. Calling me dumb was one thing. But comparing me to a Saxon was going too far. Besides, they weren't really stupid. They were the most cruel, ruthless, and vicious warriors in the world. Our uncle had been killed by one of their raiding parties, and there was talk of another invasion.

I really hated Saxons and I guess that's why I did it.

I strolled over to the railing and gave Arthur a good poke in the chest.

"CAAAAAAAAAAAAIIIIIIII!" screamed my brother.

Unfortunately, I had poked him just a little, teensy bit too hard. He tottered for a second . . . and then fell over the side of the bridge and into the rushing river below.

He wasn't supposed to fall! How dumb could you get?

I ran around the side of the bridge, but it was too late. Arthur had already gotten caught in the swift current. Panic swept through my veins. I scrambled through the bracken and raced along the shore until I saw a clump of blond hair floating in the middle of the water.

This was great, just great!

"Arthur!" I screamed.

"Help, Cai!" he answered desperately. At least he wasn't dead—yet.

That's when I heard it. It was like a thousand drums beating a death march. The roar grew and grew until it was painfully clear what it was.

Arthur was going to go over Tonkin Falls!

I was starting to catch up with him, but I had no rope to throw. There was no boat. All I could do was watch as my brother floated to his doom.

Then a miracle happened.

Someone was standing not far from the edge of the falls. A tall, thin boy wearing a strange robe was waving his arms and . . . talking to a tiny sapling. A small puff of smoke came from his hand, and I knew he must be a sorcerer!

I looked in amazement as the little tree suddenly grew up toward the sky.

The boy smiled broadly. He hadn't noticed us yet, and I could just barely hear him shout, "I did it! I did—"

But as soon as he said it something went wrong. The giant oak apparently had become too heavy for the silty soil near the river. It leaned out over the stream and, with a gigantic splash, fell into the water—right in front of Arthur!

As my brother rushed toward sure death, he grabbed on to a limb—just in the nick of time.

"Rats! . . . RATS!! . . . RAAAAATS!!!" screamed the boy, who was staring at the tree roots.

Apparently, he had no idea that he had just saved someone's life. I don't think he even saw Arthur.

"I can't do anything right!" wailed the stranger.

I was going to tell the conjurer how wrong he was, but I was still worried about my brother. I raced to the shore where the tree had fallen.

"Are you all right?" I panted as I helped Arthur onto the bank and offered him my cloak.

He was soggy and shaken, but he was alive. He was also a little angry.

"I'm fine . . . you jerk!" he shouted, pushing the cloak back in my face.

He was obviously feeling better.

I took back the heavy wool covering and climbed up the bank. Instead of arguing with my brother, I decided to thank the wizard for saving him.

The boy, who seemed to be about my age, was standing on a ledge that looked out over the falls. He stared at the water, his shoulders hunched into a tight knot.

"Hey!" I shouted.

He didn't answer.

"Hey, you!" I called several times.

Finally the stranger whirled around and glared at me. His eyes were almost too dark to see, but his skin was a sickly white. He had short brown hair and his robes had symbols and magical signs sewn on them—sort of like Merlin's, only not nearly as nice.

"I wanted to thank you for saving my brother," I said.

He looked at me with a smirk, as though he didn't believe it.

"It's true," I added.

Then he saw Arthur hobbling toward us, squeezing water out of his shirt.

"I . . . How?" he gasped.

"That tree stopped him from going over the falls. He owes his life to you."

The boy looked at the giant timber with disgust.

"That tree," he explained, "was supposed to grow over two hundred feet tall. Instead it fell over."

"Well, I'm glad it did," said Arthur. "If it hadn't I would have drowned for sure."

"This is my brother, Arthur," I said. "And I'm Cai. Actually, we both owe you a favor. If he had gotten killed it would have been my fault. I sort of pushed him off the bridge. . . . By accident, of course."

"I'm Delwid and you're welcome," replied the boy, "but saving him was also an accident. I didn't even know you were there. I was just practicing my spells."

"Practicing?" I wondered. "So you're someone's apprentice?"

Delwid let out a heavy sigh. "Not yet. The council is meeting tomorrow, and in order to get an apprenticeship I have to do one transmutation, one disappearance, and one conjuring. But I always manage to botch things up. I try to transmute a flower into a stone and it becomes a cricket. I try to make a tree grow and it falls over. . . . It's no use. I'm a failure."

"Well," said my brother, "maybe it's just the magic supplies you use. Do you have fresh Wolf's Bane or powdered Toad's Eyes?"

We knew about those from living with Merlin for the last three months.

Delwid shook his head. "I don't have any money. I've only got the stuff my father left me . . . and that's ten years old."

"Your father is a wizard?" I asked.

"Was," Delwid whispered. "He was killed in a battle when I was five. Last year I started practicing with his spells . . . but I'll never be like him."

Michael Markiewicz

Delwid turned toward the falls again, but now he moved closer to the edge. "I ought to just jump and get it over with. I'm useless." He bent his legs and swung his arms back.

Suddenly Arthur grabbed him. It was a dangerous thing to do, but Arthur seemed to enjoy perilous situations. "Wait!" he yelled as they struggled near the drop-off.

"Let me go!" screamed the boy.

"We can help you!" Arthur insisted.

"No, you can't. No one—"

"Our godfather is Merlin!"

That made Delwid stop for a second, and I helped pull him away from the falls.

"*The* Merlin?" he asked.

"The one and only," I replied, not sure what Arthur had in mind.

"Are you his apprentices?" the boy gasped.

"No, he's training us to be knights," I answered.

"But we could give you some of his supplies," said my brother with a gleam. "He buys only the best!"

"Yeah," I added. "We could—" and then I realized what Arthur was saying. "Wait a minute. We can't give away Merlin's stuff. He'll turn us into baby sparrows again."

"That doesn't sound so bad," Delwid said innocently.

"Yeah?" I snorted. "You ever had a mother

106

sparrow shove pre-digested worms down your throat?"

My point was disgustingly clear.

"But Merlin will never know," argued my brother. "We can tell him about my falling in the river and say we lost one of the bags. It would even cover up not having the mustard."

I still didn't like it. Merlin had a spooky way of finding things out.

"Besides," Arthur continued, "I owe him my life."

That much was true. We really couldn't say no.

I ran and got the four bags we had purchased and gave Delwid one that held several small pouches of supplies.

"These are fantastic!" he said, opening three of the small containers. "Wolf's Bane, real Alchemist's stones . . . and—"

"Is that all you'll need?" asked Arthur.

Delwid grinned.

"With these I could transmute a mountain into a lake!" he cried.

"Well," said Arthur, "don't get carried away. Remember, Merlin will be there."

"Will he know Delwid's using his stuff?" I asked. They were some pretty expensive supplies.

"I don't think so," answered Delwid. "As long as I don't do anything too flashy."

"Maybe you should practice some more before you go," I suggested. "These might be a little more powerful than you're used to."

Delwid examined the bags carefully. "I'll just tone it down. . . . With a little luck, nothing will go wrong this time."

That would have been nice.

Arthur and I got back to Merlin's house late that evening. We stumbled through the doorway and presented our bundles nervously. Our godfather was not happy.

"Where's the mustard!" rumbled the sorcerer as he tore open the bags and packages on his table. "And the Wolf's Bane . . . and . . ."

"Um," said Arthur.

"We, uh . . ." I added brilliantly.

"Don't make excuses!" shouted Merlin. "If there's one thing I can't stand, it's excuses."

Actually there were a lot of things Merlin couldn't stand. He couldn't stand lying. He couldn't stand being late. In fact, Arthur and I were surprisingly good at doing almost all the things that Merlin couldn't stand.

"I'm sorry, Merlin," said Arthur. "But I fell in the river and lost some of the packages."

"He almost got killed trying to save them," I added.

"Oh?" replied Merlin with a suspicious glare.

"It was just an accident," Arthur said quietly.

The wizard scowled as he studied a large spider that had crawled onto the table near the bundles.

"There are few real accidents, Arthur. People often create their own mishaps without even knowing it."

"How?" I wondered.

"Chaos is a powerful thing," he answered. "Random happenings are rarely as random as you think."

Merlin was really strange at times.

"And we're going to need those supplies tomorrow," he said in a sad, almost frightened, whisper.

Now I really felt bad.

"Maybe we can get some at the meeting tomorrow," Arthur said hopefully.

Merlin grumbled and stroked his beard, which meant there was something wrong. But he still wouldn't tell us what it was.

He looked down at the table and watched the spider climb over one of the bags of supplies.

"You'd best leave those alone," he said to the creature. "Go outside and catch some flies."

The spider immediately scurried out of the room.

"Well," the wizard said with a sigh, "at least I can still control animals. . . . Unfortunately, I can't control my dreams."

He walked into his study, where he also

slept. "You both better get some rest," he ordered. "Tomorrow is going to be a long day."

Then he shut the door softly and went to bed.

The wizard woke us early the next morning. We hardly had time to eat before we were on the road to Callen. It was a two-hour walk, and the proceeding had already started by the time we arrived.

Most of the town had come out for the annual event. Through the crowd we saw a long table with wizards seated along one side. In front of them was a large circle of people, and a boy about our age was just leaving the middle of the field.

We found a spot near where the horses were tied, but it smelled and was so thick with flies that we could hardly see. Again, one of the wretched insects flew into my ear, and Arthur laughed as I shook it out.

"You must not be keeping your ears clean, Cai," chuckled Merlin. "Flies only like things that smell!"

I didn't think it was so funny. I was going to give them both a piece of my mind, but then I spotted Delwid standing on the other side of the crowd.

"Are there any more applicants?" bellowed one of the servants.

Delwid stepped into the circle.

"You have three spells prepared?" asked a wizard at the center of the table.

Five or six other wizards sat on each side of him. They all had their casting robes on, but none looked quite as good as our godfather.

"Merlin?" asked Arthur as Delwid opened his bags and got ready. "Why aren't you one of the council?"

The great wizard smiled. "When you get to my stage in life, you don't have to do such menial tasks."

One of the wizards closest to us heard Merlin and grunted sourly.

"There are greater problems to be solved." Merlin sighed. "And it is almost time."

Then Delwid began.

"First, I will make this stone disappear," he said, pointing to a large boulder near the edge of the field.

The council stirred nervously.

"Perhaps you should try something smaller?" offered one of the sorcerers.

Delwid was too confident. He produced the appropriate spell materials and started casting.

At first it seemed to work. The huge stone slowly began to fade. But then it also started to rise into the air! It drifted up until it was nearly twenty feet over our heads. Then it vanished completely.

"See here!" said another wizard. "We can't have invisible boulders floating around. What if it should fall?"

Delwid stuttered—while the rest of us looked anxiously at the sky.

"All right," he answered quickly. "I'll turn it into a bird."

One of the wizards grimaced. "I don't know—"

But it was too late. Delwid had already pulled out the Wolf's Bane and some small stones.

"Throu An Jylat!" shouted the boy.

The sky went gray and there was a rumble of thunder. Then, out of nowhere, a strange shape began to form in the clouds. It looked like the boulder at first, but then it stretched across the horizon. It became a long thin line that bulged in the middle like a snake that had swallowed a rat. The wizards gasped as the giant thing swirled in the air and grew to the size of a house.

The ground shook and a huge mouth formed on one end of the monster. Then it became obvious what Delwid had made.

A huge black dragon spread its wings over the field and nearly blotted out the sun.

"How did he do that?" shouted the council head.

"You dolt!" screamed another.

"Lunatic!" added a third.

People scattered for cover. They ran into the forest while the wizards frantically searched their bags for something to stop the beast.

Now I knew what Merlin had been so worried about.

"It's impossible! I don't have anything nearly that potent!" cried the leader in the center.

One of them rushed over to us. "Merlin, you have to do something!" shouted the sorcerer.

That's when I first looked at our godfather. He wasn't looking at the dragon. Instead, he was staring out at the forest to the east.

"The dragon is the least of our worries. It will get worse," said Merlin.

"Worse?" asked Arthur.

"How much worse than a dragon about to devour us?" I asked.

"I could change the dragon back, but that would take time," answered Merlin. Then he pointed to the forest. "And there is a greater danger coming," he said. "I have seen it in my dreams for days."

Suddenly we heard a commotion in the forest to the east. It started with a rumbling, followed by more screaming. Only this time the screaming was coming our way.

All the people who had run off to the east were coming back in such a panic that they ran right under the wings of the giant beast without even noticing it. They rushed past us and kept going to the west!

"They're here!" shouted one.

"Run for your lives!" screamed another.

Several nearly knocked us down, and others tried to get us to follow them. But I had learned the hard way to stick by Merlin. He always seemed to know the best thing to do.

As I looked back to the east, however, I wasn't so sure. The rumbling became louder and clearer. It was the sound of men yelling and hundreds of feet trampling through the brush. Out of the trees came a large army. The soldiers wore strange armor and carried crests from unfamiliar houses. They shouted their war cries and entered the field in several lines of attack.

"Who are th—" I yelled.

"SAXONS!" screamed Arthur.

There were hundreds of them—hundreds upon hundreds. They charged forward, their swords held high, and rushed to slay all of us. The invasion had begun.

As they broke from the forest I pulled my dagger, but I knew it would do little good against their swords. Several men had already fallen at their feet, and most of the rest were fleeing for their lives. I was sure we had met our doom. If the dragon didn't kill us, the Saxons definitely would.

"What should we do?" I asked.

No one answered.

Then my brother drew his blade and stepped forward. "Merlin!" he called out. "Can you control the dragon?"

The wizard looked confused.

"The way you controlled that spider and told it to go outside and catch some flies?" Arthur added.

I didn't understand, but Merlin smiled in agreement.

"That's it!" he shouted. "Arthur, Cai, run to the middle of the field and point your daggers up at the beast. You must get the Saxons to look at it."

I didn't like it, but I knew better than to argue at a time like this.

We sprinted toward the invaders and raised our blades. Arthur and I held them there long enough to catch everyone's attention.

Then there was another miracle.

The front lines of the Saxons spotted Delwid's creation. It took a minute for all of them to see it, but the raiders finally stopped, only one hundred paces away. They stared at the dragon and then looked at us.

Merlin grinned broadly. He lifted his hands and recited a spell at the monster above us. Then he shouted something in Saxon. I didn't understand it but it didn't sound very nice.

The giant beast roared and flame shot from its snout. It reared back its ugly head and, with a mighty flap of its wings, sent a hot gust of wind across the invaders.

The warriors turned pale. Several dropped their weapons. As the beast flew down on them, the Saxon lines broke like a family of rabbits before a wolf. The dragon herded them through the forest, spraying fiery spit at them.

We could still see its dark form in the sky nearly a mile away. Later we learned that the beast continued to lunge at the Saxons while they scrambled for their boats. It kept at them as they rowed frantically to escape. Finally, as their tiny craft reached the deeper water, the spell wore off and the creature became a stone again. One of the ships was sunk by the giant boulder as it smashed right through the deck and hull.

"Merlin, you were great!" said Arthur as we listened to the Saxons' trumpets call a retreat from the bay.

"It was your quick thinking, Arthur . . . and that young boy who did it," answered the wizard. He pointed to our friend, who was still frozen with fear in the middle of the field.

"Delwid?" I wondered. "But he made that dragon by mistake. You were the one that used it to drive off the Saxons."

"So you know him!" said Merlin with a gleam. "Delwid, hmm? . . . Well," he continued as the boy stumbled toward us, "Delwid has some of the greatest magic there is. He is a chaos controller."

"A what?" asked Arthur.

"A wizard of chaos," said Merlin. "His magic uses randomness to produce just the right thing at the right time. It will probably never be what he expects, but it will always be the right thing. . . . In this case he created a dragon so that I could use it on the Saxons."

"Well, you could have just made a dragon," I said.

Merlin laughed. "If only it were that easy to make a dragon."

"You mean . . . I have powerful magic?" asked Delwid hopefully.

"Quite," answered Merlin.

"And I'm not just causing accidents all the time?"

"People often don't know what is good for them anyway," answered the wizard. "But I will recommend you for an apprenticeship." Then he looked at us. "Of course, taking my potions and giving them to an apprentice is probably a bad idea."

My knees began to shake.

Arthur's lip quivered nervously.

"Um—" started Arthur.

"You knew his name, didn't you?" Merlin asked angrily.

"Uh," I answered hopelessly.

"And it does seem strange that an apprentice would be able to afford such wonderful supplies!"

"But," I argued, "we had to give them to him . . . it was the only way to save us from those Saxons!"

"And lying about it?" replied Merlin, reaching into his wizard's sack.

"Well," said Arthur, "he saved my life."

"And that means you can steal from me?" he asked as his hands began to shape the spell.

I was going to say more, but it was too late. The magic had already taken effect. My words came out as a mere buzz.

And you wouldn't believe what flies have for dinner.

This time Henry may have bitten off more than he can chew.

FIRST KISS

Patrick Bone

Henry's face looked as white as a ghost, or maybe like he had just *seen* a ghost. He tried to hide his feelings from Katherine for fear she would make fun of him. But she read him and said, "You saw them, didn't you? I can tell by that stupid, scared look on your face. You saw them."

She was right. He had seen something. He was scared, and beginning to regret letting her talk him into going into that place.

That *place* was Hardscrabble Holler. Darkest cove in Kentucky, bragged the mountain folks who lived there. It was off-limits to kids at night. Henry couldn't recall a grown-up going into the Holler after dark, either. Except one, a long time ago. Milton Macintosh. Folks call him the Ghost of Hardscrabble Holler. Legend has it Milton was a wild sort who paid no mind to the warnings. Said a fellah should be able to hike where he pleased.

Legend also has it there wasn't much left of his body when a hunter stumbled across it a year or so after he disappeared. Some say he haunts the Holler now, warning folks to stay out. Most say it's better that way, better a ghost than alive and . . .

But Henry wasn't afraid of ghosts. No, sir. Besides, it wasn't ghosts he was warned about. The monsters of Hardscrabble Holler weren't ghosts, but *werewolves!* Every kid in the holler heard the stories. Grown-ups made sure of that.

"If'n they don't eat you," the grown-ups said, "they turn you into one of their kind."

Henry heard the story from his big brother, Bobby, who told him all about the monsters when Henry got old enough to get in trouble. Bobby said, "They live in the Holler. No one knows exactly what they look like, 'cause no one who's seen them ever came out the Holler to tell about it."

Henry remembered rolling his eyes and saying, "Yeah, sure!"

But Bobby got a serious look on his face and whispered, "They're half human, half wolf. Hunt during the full moon. Hear tell they're particularly fond of 'kid food.' Not Wheaties or oatmeal. 'Kid food,' like when I take holt a your arm and sink my teeth into it, like *this*."

Henry screamed and ran.

But that was a long time ago. Now he was twelve years old, almost a teenager. He didn't believe in werewolves. He didn't believe in any of the stuff grown-ups tell kids to keep them out of trouble. But neither did he have any desire to go down into the Holler after dark. And he never would have, either, if it hadn't been for Katherine.

Katherine believed in nothing she couldn't see with her own eyes. It was her teasing that got Henry down in Hardscrabble Holler when he should have been at home, safe and sound in his own bed. Not that the adventure was planned. Fact is, it just sort of happened.

Fall winds blew cold that October afternoon. Henry and Katherine were walking home from school together as they had since first grade, being as their cabins occupied the same ridge overlooking the few homes and business buildings in the town of Hardscrabble. They had stopped with some other kids for a soda, and now the light was fading fast, the outline of the moon already edging over the darkening mountains.

They were barely halfway home, almost to the abandoned trail leading down into the Holler, when Henry folded his arms and boasted,

"One these days, I'm gonna go on down there 'n see for myself. Yes, sir, one these days."

That's when Katherine said, "Dare you, Henry! Do it now, you got such a big mouth. Bet you're too scared go down there now."

Henry had to say it: "I ain't scared a nothing."

So that's how he found himself, on the night of the full moon, deep in Hardscrabble Holler, trying to figure out how to get out of something he never should have gotten into in the first place. And when he saw something dark and furry scurrying through the woods, he *was* scared. Not that he was going to admit it. Not to a *girl*, anyways.

That's why he said, "You stay here. I'll go into the thicket there to see if it's all clear."

He had it in mind to tell her he didn't see anything, and that they should go home because it was getting cold. That part was true. Fall nights in the mountains were cold, and they weren't dressed for a long hike. Katherine wore a cotton dress, a blue wool sweater, knee-length socks that rode down her ankles, and old high-top leather shoes like they wear in those parts. Her curly red hair blew every which way in the gusting wind.

Henry had on corduroy pants, a T-shirt, and a wool pullover sweater handed down from his

123

brother. His own leather high-tops had holes in them, and when the wind whistled through the woods, it tickled his toes. He figured freezing seemed a good enough excuse to go home. It bothered him that he had let his mouth get him into trouble. Worse, he couldn't understand why it was suddenly so important to him to show Katherine he wasn't afraid. A year ago it wouldn't have mattered what she thought of him. But now? Well, now he felt different.

That's why he scooted all by himself inside the thicket, half expecting to see something he didn't believe in. It was empty. Dark and damp, and smelling like moldy wood, but empty. Flickers of moon shadow off rhododendron branches made him shudder and think of monsters he'd seen at the movies. But there was no monster to fear. It was all just talk to scare kids into not wandering off. Or so he thought.

As he started to leave, something cold and hard grabbed his elbow. He froze, afraid to look behind him. It let go. He turned slowly to see what was there. It was Katherine, looking as scared as he was. "Darn, girl," he swore. "Your hands are cold enough to freeze fish!"

Katherine looked puzzled.

"Didn't you grab me?" he asked.

She didn't have to answer. They both heard it at once. It sounded like a sigh at first, a big sigh, low, and raspy, and long. When it inhaled, the wind whooshed through the thicket behind them. When it let out its breath, a growly, gurgly sound erupted, as if it was dripping spit and making a muddy mess on the ground.

"GRRLAUYREEXSLOCKSLUCKENSPLAT."

Henry and Katherine started shaking. They huddled so close Henry knew his mama would have spanked him if she found out. But that didn't matter just then. His attention was riveted on something in the woods next to them. Whatever was there made sloppy saliva sounds and growled like it was ready to eat.

Katherine, who always wanted to be a doctor, whispered, "I think it's got a breathing disorder, Henry."

He corrected her. "That's not a breathing disorder, Katherine. That's a *mean* disorder. Let's get out of here."

Leaving didn't seem like a big deal. The growling took place in front of them, the road home lay behind. Trying to make as little noise as possible, the two crept out of the thicket. Henry estimated they were inches from freedom when he heard another growl, this one blocking their escape.

Trying to keep his voice from breaking, he whispered, "Either that thing's a ventriloquist, or there's two of them."

Just then both ends of the thicket came alive. It seemed to Henry they were having a contest to see who could growl loudest.

"GRRLAXSPLAACHOO."

"ACHOOOORAXSPLATGRRRR."

The trees around them shook and rattled. Limbs and leaves kicked up in every direction. No one had to tell Henry they were in serious trouble.

"Sounds like they're revving their engines, getting ready to charge," he said.

Then Katherine made a face and observed, "Henry, do you need a bath, or do those things stink?"

The odor hit from both sides at once.

Henry thought it was beyond a doubt the foulest, most sickening smell he had ever inhaled.

Both kids started gagging and coughing.

"Makes skunk smell sweet," Henry gasped. "Like something dead died and needs burying . . . bad."

That's when Katherine said, "Do something!"

Henry said, "Like I'm supposed to know what."

The growling got worse. Suddenly he decided maybe it would be a good idea to make a plan.

"I know," he said, "let's run for it! I'll go this way. You go that way. We'll confuse them."

It was obvious the way Katherine grabbed his

arm that she didn't think his plan was such a good idea. "No way!" she said. "If I'm going to die, I'd just as soon die in the presence of a friend, thank you. Try again!"

This time the solution seemed to escape him, but the growling brought him to his senses.

"Okay, got a better idea. Let's break some branches and beat on them." He ripped off a mayapple switch, determined to charge.

Katherine didn't seem particularly taken with that idea, either. She grabbed him just in time.

"Henry," she said, "sometimes you aren't too bright. I think that might just make them madder."

"Okay," he said, "I'm all out of ideas, but real open to suggestions."

It was the first time he caught himself admitting that maybe a girl could think under pressure.

The look on Katherine's face told him he might be right. He knew her well enough to tell she was thinking. When she tried to figure something out, she pulled on her red hair with one hand, and stuck her thumbnail in her teeth with the other.

"Got it!" Katherine said, snapping her fingers like she just flashed on something important. "Look, Henry, those things are doing lots of growling and scratching and heavy breathing.

But they haven't attacked yet. Why do you suppose that's so?"

By the way she looked at him, Henry was sure she actually expected an answer. He was proud of how he threw it back at her. "I don't know, Katherine. Waiting for the supper bell? What do you think?"

She didn't hesitate a second. "I think they might be as afraid of us as we are of them. I think if we scared them, they'd run. It does make sense, doesn't it? They haven't attacked yet. Maybe they're just bluffing. Maybe they've got little babies and they're not feeling well. You know, maybe they're just poor little werewolves—"

"Katherine!"

She could carry on. But she did make some sense. Besides, he had nothing better to contribute. So they started to scare them.

First, they spoke nice, saying things like "Shoo, get on out of here." Then they got braver and jumped around, stomping their feet like they meant business. Pretty soon Henry almost began to enjoy it. These werewolves weren't so scary after all.

Henry invented all kinds of gruesome sounds and ugly noises. He hollered like a guinea hen being chased by a cat. He started shaking his body as if he were at a revival meeting, and tried screaming like a drunk fool on Saturday night.

It got better. Henry reached inside his shirt, cupped his hand to his armpit, and made the noises his daddy made to make his mama mad. It sounded so good on one side that he did it on the other.

When he looked over to see what Katherine was doing, he got the surprise of his life. She stood there, saying "Bad werewolves, bad werewolves," with one hand on her hip, and the other waving a finger at the thicket the way she did when she bawled out her baby brother.

Henry yelled, "You can do better than that, Katherine! Show them your bony knees. That'll scare anything off."

Katherine stopped and narrowed her eyes at him.

He stopped, too, not because she was staring at him, but because he heard . . . nothing.

No growling. No sighing. No gurgling. No sound of spit splashing on the ground. It was quiet . . . quiet, he decided, as the time Pastor Martin fell flat asleep during his own sermon.

They waited.

One minute.

Two.

Three.

"They're gone," he whispered.

Katherine nodded.

"Let's get!" he said.

She nodded harder.

They took three steps, and that's when he heard something.

His heart stopped.

Silence.

He looked at Katherine.

She was shaking as much as he was.

Then he heard it one more time and cocked his head, a puzzled look on his face. "Sounds like a chuckle," he whispered.

Katherine said, "A what?"

"A chuckle. You know, a little laugh."

Katherine shrugged her shoulders and said, "Wonder what they're about, Henry?"

"They're toying with us," he said.

The laughter suddenly got louder and bigger and crazier. To Henry it sounded like a cross between a jackass and the uncle Henry after whom he was named. The creatures laughed so hard he could almost see them holding their bellies with tears in their eyes. They kept moving around, crashing through the underbrush, seeming to fall all over themselves. It occurred to Henry they must be laughing so hard they couldn't stand straight.

The werewolves were laughing and laughing.

And the two kids were running and running.

They didn't need a path out of the thicket.

They made their own, circling wide away from the trail. They ran through the trees and over bushes, ruined their shoes in mud holes, ripped their clothes on thorn trees. But they kept running. At the railroad tracks they were halfway home. But they didn't stop, not even to look behind them.

After he splashed through the creek leading into town, Henry pulled up to catch his breath. When he looked around, he couldn't find Katherine.

His heart sank. Suddenly he admitted to himself that she was more than just the tomboy next door. He felt confused and hurt, and caught himself fearing for a friend who seemed all of a sudden closer than just a friend. He wiped away a tear that slipped from his eye and squared his shoulders. He would go back for her. No matter the danger, he would rescue Katherine. That's when he saw her walk out of the woods just below the creek.

His face flushed. It came to him that maybe he should take back some of the mushy stuff he had just admitted. But there wasn't time to dwell on it.

"Come on!" he called. "We still got a ways to go before we're safe."

They hurried past Miller's barn, Hansen's Garage, old lady Larsen's place, and finally, back to the schoolyard. It wasn't home, but it was familiar. Exhausted, they collapsed on the merry-go-round.

After a while Katherine pointed her toe into the dirt and pushed the merry-go-round.

Henry pushed, too.

Soon they floated in gentle circles, like a couple of schoolkids—which they were. The full moon shone through the tall trees around the grounds. It seemed safe there in the school-yard. Henry admitted to himself how warm and even a little mushy he felt sitting close to Katherine. That's when she turned toward him and he discovered he couldn't take his eyes off hers.

We're older now, he thought. *I'm twelve, not a kid anymore. If I'd had to, I* would *have saved her from the werewolves*. It occurred to him that if he had the courage for that, he was sure brave enough to give Katherine a kiss, his first kiss.

He snuggled up to her, slipped one arm around her, and said, "Well, Katherine, we sure handled that, now, didn't we?"

His face was inches from hers.

I'm gonna do it, he thought. Now or never. He licked his lips and was just about to smack the big one home when she threw back her head and started to laugh.

"We sure did. We sure did. We scared them all right. Let's do it again. How about it,

Henry? Moon's still full. How 'bout we go back and do it again?"

Henry wondered if maybe the thought of him kissing her hadn't sent Katherine into shock. "You okay, Katherine?" he asked.

She didn't answer. She just stared at him for a moment with a vacant look in her eyes, then started to laugh again. Only this time, Henry knew she wasn't laughing at something he was about to do.

She moved closer and reached up with her mouth like *she* was going to kiss *him.*

That's when he saw something that sent a shiver down his back. That's when he saw the lacerations at the base of her neck.

He felt his blood turn cold as Katherine put a hand to her throat and touched the deep wounds that raked her skin. For a moment she stared at the blood on her fingertips.

When she spoke again, her voice sounded different. "Full moon, Henry. We gotta go back now. Do it again. Next full moon, too, and the one after that, and after that."

Henry couldn't speak, couldn't move. The look in Katherine's eyes held him paralyzed.

She put her arms around him, drew him closer, and growled, "Now, weren't you about to kiss me?"

Seeing is believing ... sometimes.

OPTICAL ILLUSION

Mack Reynolds

Molly brought my plate, silver, and side dishes and placed them before me without fuss or comment. I was an old customer, and one of the things I liked about Molly was that she never fussed over me.

I usually make a practice of eating after the rush hour, but today I was early and the restaurant crowded. It was only a matter of time before someone would want to share my table.

I didn't look up when he asked, "Is this seat taken?" His voice was high, almost to the point of shrillness, in spite of his attempt to control it.

"No," I told him, "go right ahead."

He hung his cane, or umbrella, whatever it was, over the back of his chair and fumbled his hat underneath it before climbing to his seat.

Then he picked up the menu from where it stood between the catsup and napkins.

"Nothing fit to eat," he muttered finally.

I said, "The pot pie is quite good today."

Molly came up and he said to her, "I'll have the Swiss steak, miss. Green peas, french fries. I'll decide on the dessert later."

"Coffee?"

"Milk."

I don't know what it was that first gave me the idea that the person seated across the table from me wasn't a midget at all. Not a midget or dwarf, but a child pretending adulthood and doing a fantastically good job of it. As I say, I don't know what it was that gave me the hint, possibly I'm more susceptible to such intuitiveness than the next man.

But whatever it was, he knew almost as soon as I did.

That is, he knew that I'd caught on to him, and somehow it frightened me. The whole idea was so bizarre—a child, not yet in his teens, passing himself off, for some reason of his own, as a mature, if stunted, adult.

"So," he said, his shrill voice almost a hiss. He put down his fork. "So . . ."

How can I describe that cold voice? The voice of a child . . . but not a child. Not a child as we know one.

I reached for the sugar, which was there

where it always is at the end of the table next to the salt and pepper and the mustard jar. I measured out a spoonful very carefully without looking up at him. As I have said, somehow I was afraid.

He said, still softly, "So at last a stupid human has penetrated my disguise."

A *human*, he had said.

His voice was a child's, but his words dug into me viciously. "Ah, so that surprises you, my curious friend. You wonder, eh?" There was a sneering quality now, a contemptuous overtone.

I cleared my throat, tried to cover my confusion by taking a gulp of the coffee. "I don't know what you mean . . . sir."

He chuckled and mimicked, "I don't know what you mean . . . sir." Then his voice snapped over at me, even as he kept his tone low. "Why did you hesitate before adding the *sir*, eh? Why?" He didn't wait for an answer. "I'll tell you why. Because somehow you've discovered that my age is less than I would have it known."

He was boiling with rage, and in spite of his size and the public nature of our whereabouts, I was afraid of him. Why, I didn't know. Somehow I sensed that—impossibly—he could destroy me at will.

I fumbled my cup back into its saucer, kept my face averted.

"You're terrified," he snapped again. "You recognize your master even as you wonder about him."

"My master?" I said. Who did he think . . .

"Your master," he repeated. "Mankind's master. The new race. The super-race, *Homo superior,* if you will. He is here, my snooping friend, and you, you and your stupid nation-divided, race-divided, class-divided, religion-divided humanity will never stand before him."

It was hard for me to assimilate. I had come into my favorite restaurant for my midday meal. It had been a routine day, and I had expected it to continue as one. Now, I had been startled so many times in the past few minutes that I felt I was in a state of shock.

"Oh, it's been suggested before," he went on, seemingly welcoming this opportunity to explain to me, to gloat over me. "The possibility that mutations would develop, a super-race, a super-humanity as far above man as man is above the ape."

"How . . . what . . ."

He cut me off. "What difference if it was the atomic bomb, laboratory experiments, or only nature's continual plodding advance? The fact remains, we are here, a considerable number of us, and in a few years, when we have developed our full capacities, man will hear from us. Ah, how he will hear!"

Long ago an icy hand had gripped my heart. Now it squeezed.

"Why," I stumbled. "Why tell me all this? Surely you wouldn't disguise yourself if you didn't wish to keep it all a secret."

He laughed mockingly. There was still much of the immature in him, super-race or nay.

"Because it doesn't make any difference," he whispered. "None at all. Ten minutes from now, you will remember nothing of this conversation. Hypnotism, my stupid *Homo sapiens*, can be a developed art when practiced on the lower orders."

His voice went hard and incisive. "Look up into my eyes," he ordered.

I had no power to resist. Slowly my face came up. I could *feel* his eyes drill into mine.

"This you will forget," he ordered. "All of this conversation, all of this experience, you will forget."

He came to his feet, took his time about securing his things, and then left.

Molly came over later. "Gee," she said, "that little midget that was just here, he sure tips good."

"I would imagine," I told her. I was still shaken. "He probably has a substantial source of income."

"Oh," Molly said, making conversation as she cleaned up. "You been talking to him?"

"Yes," I told her, "we had quite a discussion." I added thoughtfully, "And as a result I have duties to perform."

I came to my own feet and reached up for my hat and cane, where they hung on their usual hook.

I thought: *possibly man has more of a chance than these hidden enemies realize. Mental powers beyond us they may have, although they would seem lacking in the more kindly qualities. But this one hadn't been as sharp as he liked to think himself. Hypnotic powers he might possess beyond our understanding, but that didn't prevent him from making a very foolish error. He hadn't caught on to the fact that I'm blind.*

*Mary Downing Hahn provides our second
Scottish sea monster for this collection—and
with it a chance to point something out. You
see, one of the questions beginning writers
ask most often is "What if someone steals my
idea?" But the truth is, fine writers often
come up with similar ideas. The people who
worry about this don't realize that what
counts more than the idea is what you do
with it!*

*That's one reason I'm including two Scottish
sea monster stories in this book—so you can
see that when two fine writers both work with
the same material, what you get is two
completely different stories.*

*(But the main reason is I liked both stories,
and didn't want to give one up!)*

TROUBLE AFOOT

Mary Downing Hahn

I'd been walking for several hours, enjoying the
spring sunshine and paying little attention to
the time, when the balmy weather suddenly
changed. Black clouds raced across the sky,

darkening the green countryside. Trees shuddered in the rising wind, turning their leaves so the white undersides showed. Thunder rumbled, peal after peal, coming closer and closer. Lightning shot toward earth, forking downward as if flung by Zeus's invisible hand.

As the first drops of rain struck me, I looked about, hoping to spot a signpost, but the thickening gloom made it impossible to see more than a few feet in any direction. If only I'd paid more attention to my map and compass before it grew too dark to read them. Father had warned me to navigate carefully. "This is the first time you've walked to your uncle's cottage by yourself," he'd said. "The paths across the moors twist and turn. It's easy for an inexperienced hiker to lose his way."

Much as I hated to admit it, I should have heeded his advice. Instead I'd dillied and dallied along, never doubting I was following the route Father had carefully mapped out for me.

Only the prospect of facing Father's scorn gave me the courage to continue my journey. If I showed up on our doorstep, soaked and bedraggled, whimpering like a scared puppy, he and Mother might forbid me to go off on my own again.

Shouldering my rucksack, I followed the path down a steep hill and into a densely wooded valley. I knew the danger of taking shelter under a tree, yet it wasn't the wind or the lightning, fearsome as they were, that frightened me most. What made my heart pound were the strange sounds I heard beneath the storm's roar—growlings and mutterings, thrashings in the underbrush, muffled cries, a scream almost human in its terror.

How often had Father chided me for my nervous imaginings? Even Mother, usually so kind and understanding, had lately grown tired of my fears. Indeed, I was convinced the pair of them had allowed me to undertake the ten-mile trek in hope the experience would strengthen me in mind as well as in body.

To keep the monsters of my imagination at bay, I concentrated on the pleasant weekend I planned to spend with my uncle, an intelligent and witty fellow, always eager to tell a joke or play a merry trick—so different from his brother, my stern and humorless father. A few days earlier I'd received a letter in which he mentioned finding something of great scientific importance in a nearby lake. "I shan't tell you what it is," he'd written. "You'll have to come down and see for yourself, my boy. Suffice it to say, you'll be just as thrilled as I am."

Because I shared Uncle Bert's lifelong interest in marine biology, I'd used every wile to persuade my parents I was old enough, strong enough, smart enough, and brave enough to find my way to my uncle's. I couldn't turn back now.

So on I went, slogging steadfastly through rivulets of rainwater in what I hoped was the right direction. Shivering with cold, I yearned for the sight of my uncle's cozy cottage, a cup of tea, and a warm seat by the fire.

When I'd all but convinced myself I'd taken a wrong turn somewhere along the way, I saw a light flickering in the window of a small cottage set well back from the road. "Uncle Bert!" I cried, running down the muddy lane. "Uncle Bert, it's me, William. I'm finally here!"

My uncle did not appear, nor did he answer my calls. I bounded up the front steps, thinking he must not have heard me. To my surprise, the door was wide open. The lantern hanging in the open window swung wildly, casting moving shadows over broken furniture and scattered books and papers. Water puddled the floor, giving off the stench of rotten fish. Worst of all, I saw no sign of my uncle.

Cautiously I stepped inside, half hoping I was the victim of one of his strange tricks. "Uncle Bert?" I called softly.

There was no answer.

Summoning the little courage I possessed, I went to the hearth, grabbed the poker, and, with my back to the wall, assumed what I hoped was a threatening pose. "Is anyone here?" I whispered in a voice croaking with fear.

Outside, the wind shrieked, rain rattled against the roof, trees creaked and groaned. Inside, nothing stirred, no one spoke.

Yet I couldn't stop trembling. It seemed something had burst into my uncle's cozy cottage and torn it apart. Though I neither saw nor heard it, I felt the intruder's presence all around me. Perhaps it was still outside, circling the cottage, watching me, biding its time. I ran to the window and slammed it shut, threw myself at the door, and bolted it fast.

"Uncle Bert, Uncle Bert!" I cried. "Where are you? What happened here?"

As before, the only reply was the mournful wailing of the wind.

Nearly mad with fear and worry, I took a deep breath and forced myself to think of Father. What would that paragon of reason say if he were here? Picturing his stern face, I closed my eyes and told myself I must control my imagination. If I did not, I would most certainly lose my sanity.

There were several possibilities. Perhaps, as I'd first thought, Uncle Bert had staged the scene himself and was at this moment hiding somewhere, watching me with glee. Cautiously I opened the door and poked my head out into the driving rain. "Enough is enough,

Uncle Bert. Your trick worked marvelously well," I called. "You can come back now."

Though I waited several minutes, the kindly face I hoped to see did not appear.

Once more I bolted the door. Another possibility remained. Uncle Bert had gone out to enjoy the spring sunshine earlier in the day. Not expecting bad weather, he'd neglected to close the door and windows when he left. While he was gone, the storm struck, making it impossible for him to return. He might have sought shelter in the nearby village. In his absence the wind and rain had rushed through the cottage, toppling furniture, scattering papers and books, flooding the floor.

Calmed somewhat, I turned my attention to the disorder surrounding me. To help my uncle, as well as to occupy myself, I mopped up the foul-smelling water, righted the furniture, and stacked his scattered papers and notebooks in neat piles. When I'd done all I could, I made myself comfortable in a chair by the fire and waited for my uncle to come through the door, laughing and apologizing for his absence.

Minutes passed, then hours, ticked and chimed by the old clock on the mantel. The longer I waited, the more apprehensive I became. Where was my uncle? When would he appear?

To keep my morbid fears from returning, I

went to the table where I'd stacked my uncle's notebooks and began leafing through them, hoping to find a reference to the discovery he'd mentioned in his letter. I skimmed pages of exquisitely drawn pen and ink sketches of various marine creatures. The accompanying notes detailed the life cycles of mollusks and anemones, of crustaceans, of fish both large and small. *Well done,* I thought, *but nothing out of the ordinary.*

But what was this? I stared, transfixed, at a drawing of what appeared to be an enormous prehistoric beast, something long since extinct, yet drawn with such vivid detail it seemed to spring to life before my very eyes. Pages of dense notes accompanied the monstrous picture. Written in my uncle's cramped penmanship, they were impossible to read in the dim light of the fire.

Fetching the lantern from its hook, I bent over the notebook. As I slowly deciphered my uncle's handwriting, I realized I was reading an account of his first glimpse of the monster he'd drawn so carefully. If one could believe what he'd written, Uncle Bert had been caught in a storm near the lake behind the cottage. Taking shelter in the trees, he was astonished to see the head and neck of a huge serpent emerge from the water.

"The creature," he wrote, "is unlike anything I've ever seen or read about. Its neck is long and slender, its jaws huge, its teeth fearsome. Dark brown in color, and covered with scales, I estimate it to be over a hundred feet in length. Although it did not look at me, it seemed to sense it was being watched, and dove into the depths of the lake, leaving behind a noxious odor. At this point, I do not know if the beast is hostile or benign, but I intend to continue my observations."

I read and reread Uncle Bert's words, shaking my head in disbelief. Was this a hoax? Or had he fallen prey to the same sort of nightmarish delusions I sometimes suffered?

Filled with dread, I continued reading. "A pattern is beginning to emerge," Uncle Bert wrote after several more sightings. "The creature appears only in rainy weather. Perhaps storms disturb its rest. Despite what I've heard from the local people, I must go closer if I am to learn more about the creature's nature. I shall write to William tomorrow and invite him to share my excitement!"

On the next page Uncle Bert's handwriting grew extremely difficult to read. He seemed to be highly agitated, nervous, possibly frightened. A phrase here, a word there. "It's seen me . . . hostile, I fear . . . danger . . . The old tales are right, I should have listened . . . must warn William, must tell him not to . . ."

Large wavering words ran across the wet paper: "Rain and wind tonight, rain and wind. Not safe here after all, not safe anywhere ..."

I dropped the notebook and turned fearfully to the window. Outside the wind still blew fiercely, driving rain against the glass, breaking branches, toppling trees, howling like a beast circling the cottage.

Not safe here, Uncle Bert had written, *not safe anywhere.* What had he meant? Where had he gone? Had he run off into the storm, seeking safety in the village? Or had the creature ... No, the possibility was too horrible to contemplate. It had to be a prank—but no, it was so vivid, so real, it had to be true.

I do not wish to dwell upon the hours I spent alone in that cottage, pacing the floor, too terrified to sleep, veering back and forth between belief and disbelief. I shall merely say it was, till then at least, the worst night of my life.

When morning finally came, I opened the door and peered outside. Although the storm's fury had abated, rain still fell steadily and the wind made a desolate sound in the trees.

In the gray light of day, my fears suddenly seemed absurd. Surely I hadn't actually believed my uncle's story! The notebook and all it contained was just the sort of prank Uncle Bert delighted in playing. He was probably on his way to the cottage now, chuckling every step of the way. Indeed, I could almost hear him say, "Well, well, I fooled you, my boy! I hope you weren't too frightened!"

I had no intention of letting my uncle get away with his trick. He'd gone too far this time. Grabbing an oilskin jacket from a peg by the door, I decided to go in search of him. "A sea serpent!" I'd exclaim when we met. "Did you actually expect to scare me with such childish nonsense?"

If, as I surmised, Uncle Bert had spent the night in the village, he'd most likely return by way of the lake. I set out cheerfully, planning to take a narrow path I remembered from a previous visit. To my surprise, I found myself following a wide swath of uprooted trees and shrubbery cutting through the woods from the cottage to the lake. *Evidence of the storm's strength*, I thought, marveling at the power of nature.

I called my uncle once or twice, but he didn't answer. Indeed, nothing responded, not even a bird. Except for the wind and the rain, the woods were utterly silent. My voice echoed and re-echoed, bouncing from tree to tree, now ahead, now behind.

By the time I reached the lake, the forest's gloom had dampened my spirits to such an extent that I was on the verge of surrendering to my fears of the night before. Longing to see my uncle, I stood on the shore and gazed on a scene as desolate as any I'd ever seen. The water was dark and murky, and the far shore was shrouded in sheets of rain, giving the lake the boundless immensity of the sea itself.

Feeling as if I'd come to the edge of the known world, I stepped back and heard something crunch under my heel. At my feet, I saw my uncle's glasses. The lenses were broken, the frame twisted. His tweed cap lay a few inches away. A hiking boot in the style he fancied floated near shore. But, worst of all, I saw marks in the sand that could have been made by one thing and one thing only—a man's heels as he was dragged, still struggling, into the lake's dark depths.

What had taken place here was no joke, no lighthearted prank. A hideous scene rose before my unwilling eyes—Uncle Bert struggling, calling for help, caught in the coils of the serpent he'd observed so carefully.

Afraid to turn my back, I began edging away from the lake. But before I reached the forest, the water began to churn. Waves rose. Surf washed over my boots. The wind shrieked. Rain lashed my face like a stinging whip. Even though I had no wish to see what was causing the disturbance, I could not run. I might as well have been made of stone.

Suddenly a huge snake-like head erupted

from the middle of the lake. Draped with sheets of foul-smelling algae and weeds, it rose higher and higher above the waves. From some distance it turned its long neck and fixed its gaze on me. How long those eyes stared into mine I do not know, but I felt as if I were doomed to stand forever on the shore of that infernal lake, the object of a fearful scrutiny.

Then, as quickly as it appeared, the creature sank into the black water and vanished. Like a man released from a spell, I turned and ran, taking the path the monster itself had made as it pushed its way through the woods last night, seeking my poor uncle.

Bypassing the cottage, I took the road to a village a mile or so to the south. Let the police go there to collect the evidence. I had no wish to revisit the scene. My rucksack was of no importance to me now. Neither were my uncle's notebooks.

At the police station, the constable looked up from his papers, obviously startled by my appearance. "What's the trouble, young man?" he asked.

"The trouble is," I gasped, barely able to speak, "the trouble is—Uncle Bert has disappeared."

"Bert Pinkham?" the constable asked. "The chap who moved into Oak Cottage a couple of months ago?"

"Yes," I whispered. "Last night, something

... something ..." I stopped, afraid to tell this sensible pipe-smoking chap what I'd seen. He'd think me mad.

"Start at the beginning," the constable advised. "There's a good lad."

Trying to speak in a normal voice, I said, "When I arrived last night, the cottage was in disarray and my uncle was missing. This morning, I found some of his belongings beside the lake. I saw footprints, and then I saw, then I—" Unable to continue, I burst into tears.

"I knew trouble was afoot last night," the constable said. "What with the storm and all. Sensed it coming, I did."

His voice trailed away as he fumbled with his pipe. "I warned your uncle not to meddle with it," he went on. "But he wouldn't listen. No, sir, he insisted on studying it. Spied on it. Drew pictures. Didn't give it a moment's peace."

I gazed at the constable, too frightened to defend Uncle Bert. It was clear the man knew more about the thing in the lake than I did. No doubt, he also knew exactly what end my poor uncle had met on that desolate shore.

"It likes its privacy," the constable added. "It don't care to be looked at, it don't care to be watched. If a cow or a sheep disappears, no one in these parts makes a fuss. We have the sense to let it be."

"But surely—" I began, only to be interrupted.

"Lord help you if it catches you looking at it!" the constable cried, striking the desk with one fist.

Remembering the creature's dark and terrible stare, I began to tremble. "What do you mean, sir?"

"Why, if it catches you looking at it, you're a goner! The creature won't rest till it tracks you down. No matter how far you run or how fast, lad, it'll find you."

Somehow I got to my feet. Ignoring the constable's request to sit down and fill out some forms, I ran from his office.

Since that day I've had no rest, no peace. I dare not sleep or sit down to enjoy a meal or return home for fear of endangering my poor parents. I run, walk, and stumble through towns and villages. People look at me, they wonder, they call me mad. Some laugh, some jeer. Others draw away in fright.

Only I and I alone hear that hideous sloshing, sucking sound beneath the wind, beneath the rain. Closer it comes and closer. My nose burns with the stench of rotting fish, my skin is cold and clammy.

Oh, it would be better to be mad than to know what follows me!

*We started this book with a story about little
monsters. Now meet Jocelyn, a little monster
of a completely different kind.*

VEND U.

Nancy Springer

We did not like Jocelyn.

Jocelyn put tapioca pudding in our bookbags.
Jocelyn put Jell-O in our gym shoes. Jocelyn
smeared Ben-Gay on toilet seats. In the boys'
room, too. And if we were on a field trip and
we all went into a convenience store to get
snacks, Jocelyn would find whipped cream and
squirt it all over the store and we'd all get
kicked out and nobody would get any snacks.

Jocelyn parked chewing gum on people's
heads. Jocelyn parked boogers on locker
handles.

Jocelyn beat people up. Boys, too.

If we drew faces in art class, Jocelyn would
reach over and turn the noses into vacuum
cleaners.

157

We did not like Jocelyn. We stayed away from her. Nobody was her friend.

So at first we were kind of glad about what happened with Jocelyn and the monster vending machine.

It was summertime. It should have been vacation from you-know-who. But our parents sent us to this summer arts day camp on a college campus and there she was. Jocelyn.

Nobody wants to get sued, so forget the name of the college. Let's just call it Vend U.

The college kids who were there for sports practice were so big they reached right over our heads in the lunch line. The campus was big. The buildings were big. But the vending machines were the biggest of all. In the cafeteria there was a whole wall that was nothing but vending machines standing shoulder to shoulder like huge metal football linebackers in black uniforms. With no heads. Humongous. Jocelyn was as tall as any of us, but she could just about reach the coin slots.

Right away she shoved in front of everybody. Of course we were all crowded in front of the vending machines. Like, arts camp is okay, but vending machines are vending machines are LIFE. And we had never seen so many vending machines that sold so much STUFF. Not just candy and chips and soda and gum but coffee and ice cream and turkey dinner seafood cocktail buffalo wings buffet. And not just awesome stuff to eat but nail clippers Swiss Army spy cameras poker baseball fishing hats Parcheesi sets harmonicas rubber stamp printing presses folding bikes trips to Disney World. We all stood bug-eyed with our mouths airing out, looking at that whole wall of hard plate-glass bellies full of coiled metal guts with wonderful stuff in them, but Jocelyn didn't waste any time looking.

Jocelyn just tossed her head and got moving. Jocelyn was a tough slim girl like a motor always running, and when something made her stop she made noise. Right away Jocelyn ran all along the whole row of machines smacking her hands against all the buttons at once. She didn't put any money in, just whacked buttons.

"Stop it, Jocelyn!" somebody yelled.

Whenever anybody tried to tell Jocelyn anything, she always grinned like a snake and whipped her head back and cranked open her mouth, which was always slimed with green bubble gum, and started to sing. What was really annoying was that she always sang the same thing. Which was what she did right then. She sang, "Don't worry, be HAPPY," and she kept right on punching buttons.

"Stop it! They don't like it!" about six of us yelled at once.

Which is weird, that we all yelled it at once, but we all felt it. The vending machines didn't like it that Jocelyn disrespected them. They were big and tall with chests that stuck out even harder than Arnold Schwarzenegger's and they didn't like it at all.

Right in the center was a monster candy machine, the biggest vending machine of all, with one of those liquid-crystal displays that do words, like TRY DOUBLE-YUMMEE NEW TEABERRY GUM. Usually those displays stay sort of dark greenish all the time. But when Jocelyn didn't put any money in and whammed the Butterfinger buttons (F8) and the Nestlé's Crunch buttons (G10) at the same time, the display started to glow yellow, not happy yellow but a kind of watch-out yellow.

"Stop that," a girl said to Jocelyn.

"Get out of the way," a boy said. He had two quarters. "I want to buy something." Of course he wanted to use the machine Jocelyn was at.

And of course Jocelyn couldn't let somebody else go first. "Don't worry, be happy," she sang, and she whipped out a big coin purse stuffed full of money. She plunked two quarters into the monster candy machine and jabbed the Kit Kat buttons about five times as hard as she would have had to.

The yellow screen started flashing a black word: OWWW. At the same time the Kit Kat metal coil turned, which was what was expected, and next would come the *thunk* as the candy bar fell into the grab slot. Which it did. Except there were two thunks. *Thunk thunk.* And we could see through the glass. We all saw. *Two* candy bars fell.

"Lucky!" we yelled, and we were not happy that Jocelyn had gotten two candy bars, because after all, weren't we nicer kids than she was? Then we all crowded forward to try and see if the vending machine would give us two candy bars, too. Jocelyn was quicker. She snatched her candy bars and jammed two more quarters into the coin slot and whammed the buttons.

GREEDY, AREN'T WE? the machine flashed, and now the display was traffic-light red. But it did it again. *Thunk thunk.* Two Kit Kat bars.

"Happy," Jocelyn sang, "be HAPPEEEEE," and fast as fate, keeping control of the machine, she grabbed her candy bars and slammed in more quarters and hit the buttons again.

Nothing happened. No *thunk thunk.* Not even one *thunk.*

"Hey!" Jocelyn yelled. "Where's my candy?"

The display, which had gone sundown purple, flashed YOU'LL GET FAT.

"Hey!" Jocelyn started trying to shake the machine, which was so big and heavy she couldn't rock it. "Gimme my candy bars!"

Meanwhile some of us had moved off to the other machines, and we were kind of disgusted when we would get just one soda or whatever we paid for instead of two. But we were still watching Jocelyn shaking the candy machine. "For crying out loud, Jocelyn," somebody said, "you've already got more candy than you put in money for."

YOU'LL GET CAVITIES, the machine told her.

Jocelyn just got real mad. "I don't care!" She started pounding on the machine with her fists, and Jocelyn knew how to hit hard. "Gimme my candy!" *Wham,* she pounded, *wham wham wham.*

PARDON ME. The machine's display had gone pure velvety black with icy white letters.

"Jocelyn, stop it," somebody said. "You're gonna get in trouble."

But the vending machine turned its big steely Kit Kat coil just a little bit. Just enough to let one Kit Kat bar slip down and hang from the tip of the coil by a corner of its wrapper, dangling behind the glass.

"You snothead!" Jocelyn stopped pounding on the vending machine and stood panting. "You big fat buttface!" She got down on her knees, bent over, and stuck her arm into the

grab slot up to her elbow. She was trying to reach all the way up inside the machine and grab that Kit Kat bar. We could see her hand wiggling around like a lizard or something inside the glass at the very bottom edge. But she needed about eight or ten more inches to get to the Kit Kat bar. She scrooched down closer to the slot and twisted around and got her arm in there up to the shoulder and her hand snaked farther into the machine.

Just as her fingertips touched that Kit Kat bar, all the metal coils sprang forward and grabbed her. All at the same time. We saw it. Her fingers shot wide open as those coils clamped on to her arm. And at the same time that grab slot changed shape and opened up like a happy metal mouth, like a giant baby's mouth about to latch on to a monster pacifier or something. It all happened so fast that Jocelyn didn't even get time to scream before her head disappeared into that vending machine and that big metal mouth was slurping in the rest of her like it was inhaling a milk shake.

A few kids screamed, but mostly we were all so surprised and fascinated that we hardly even made a noise, we just gawked. Anyway, it wasn't like it mattered enough to scream about. This was Jocelyn.

Maybe we should have tried to help. Like,

we could have grabbed her by the legs and pulled her out. But we didn't.

The plate of glass went dark for a minute. And Jocelyn's legs disappeared and then her feet and the whole huge vending machine shuddered and shook. We all jumped back. But then the glass cleared up, and everything looked just like before, Mr. Goodbar Rolos Raisinets M&M's Snickers—except Jocelyn was gone.

The vending machine's display was a serene green. It said *URP*.

We all started talking at once and some of us flopped down to look under the machine— somebody found a nickel that was practically welded to the sticky linoleum, it had been there so long—and some of us ran to look behind the machine. The whole row of machines had a gray dusty space behind it, and we looked in there. But all we saw was cruddy electric cables and pipes and stuff. Jocelyn wasn't there.

Jocelyn wasn't anywhere.

"Well, good," some kid said. "No more Jocelyn."

Of course that was what we all were thinking, but most of us didn't want to say it because we were nice kids. But when somebody said it we all yelled, "Yeah!"

"No more tapioca pudding!"

"Or boogers!"

"No more Jocelyn boogers!"

"Jocelyn's gone!"

"Good!"

We all yelled and laughed. But nobody took her Kit Kat bars or her money. There were four Kit Kat bars and a coin purse lying on the floor in front of the biggest vending machine. We all looked at them but nobody touched them. They lay there all day.

Everything was okay—in fact everything was spiffy diffy for a little while—until adults started wondering what had happened to Jocelyn.

It took a few days. At first when the teachers noticed that Jocelyn was missing, which of course they noticed right away because things got so peaceful for a change, they didn't want to know where she was. They wanted to think she was somewhere else she was supposed to be, like she went home sick or she was absent or she was visiting somebody else's class. And her parents—Jocelyn always said whenever her parents grounded her it only lasted one day before they couldn't stand having her around— even her parents wanted to think she was somewhere else, like staying with a friend. Yeah, right, like she had any friends. But that was what they wanted to think.

So things were great for a couple of days. No

Jocelyn. But then the cops came and started asking questions.

Then it got really uncomfortable. Because, you know, what were we supposed to tell them? So we told them we didn't know anything. Then we felt bad, which was stupid, because we hadn't done anything to Jocelyn, but we felt bad anyway because we'd lied. Then because we felt bad we looked guilty and the teachers and cops and people saw us looking guilty and kept asking questions harder and getting more and more annoying until it almost would have been better having Jocelyn around again.

When things reached that point, which was when Jocelyn had been gone a week, we knew we had to try to do something.

We hadn't gone near the vending machines since it happened. If teachers and cops had a clue about kids at all they should have known where to look just because we were eating the cafeteria food and not going near the vending machines.

But a week after the monster vending machine's revenge on Jocelyn we all went over there after lunch. It wasn't like we decided. We just did it. One of us went over to look and then we all went over to look.

We gathered at a safe distance from the machines, like ten or twelve feet, which was still nearer than we'd been since it happened. We stood there and jiggled our feet and stuff but nobody said anything. Nobody did anything. Nobody knew what to do.

The biggest vending machine's liquid crystal display started to glow a sunny color with black letters flashing across it, like there was a new kind of candy being advertised.

So of course we had to see what it said. It was like vending machine gravity took hold. We weren't thinking about Jocelyn anymore; we just fingered the dimes and quarters in our pockets. We just wanted to slip them into the slots. We wanted to hear those wonderful sounds, *click chinggg whirrrr grunk.* And the *thunk* of a vendable being vended. We wanted to grab something out of the grab slot. We wanted to check the coin returns.

We were nice kids; would the vending machines eat us?

We all inched forward with our necks stretched so we didn't have to get too close before we could read the black letters.

On a mellow yellow background the biggest vending machine was saying, DON'T WORRY.

All of a sudden we all started smiling and laughing because everything was all right; the biggest vending machine was our friend. The biggest vending machine forgave us for being of the same species as Jocelyn. Life was good; we could buy candy bars again. O great vending machine, thankyou thankyou. We all crowded around to drool over the NutRageous bars, the Starbursts, the Almond Joys, the—

"Whoa!" somebody yelled.

There behind the glass, between the 5th Avenue bars and the 100 Grands, was a miniature Jocelyn looking out at us.

Really looking. The eyes watched us. It wasn't like a toy or a doll. It was real. It was exactly like Jocelyn.

We all jumped back and we all started talking so loud and so fast and we were all so discombobulated that we still don't understand exactly what happened next. Nobody will admit to it, but maybe one of us was actually crazy enough to put money in. Like, a mini Jocelyn only cost ten cents and some of us were saying hey, get her out of there so the cops don't see her, but we hadn't actually taken a vote or anything, we were still milling around and babbling when—

Click. Chinggg. Whirrr. Grunk. We all heard the sounds of money in the big machine's belly, the mechanism starting to move. We all gasped and watched, quiet as bunnies.

Thunk thunk.

We all saw. Not one Jocelyn, but two Jocelyns, toppled out of the coil and into the grab slot.

We all stepped back. Nobody reached to pull them out.

Nobody needed to. They came crawling out all by themselves.

BE HAPPY the machine flashed.

We weren't happy. We were way far the opposite of happy. We were so far unhappy that we couldn't move, we couldn't scream, we couldn't run. We just watched pop-eyed like frogs as the little teensy hands hauled the metal flap back so the heads and bodies could struggle out. Good grief, Jocelyn was strong. Jocelyns. Plural. They snaked out of that slot like Marines out of the jungle, swung their legs over the edge, hung by their hands for just an eyeblink, and dropped to the linoleum floor.

Then, the instant their feet hit the floor, they grew. Quickly. They shot up like inflatables until they were Jocelyn-sized again.

We were all backing away, but not fast enough. Right away, without even saying hi, both Jocelyns grabbed the nearest kids. One Jocelyn grabbed a girl and the other one grabbed a boy.

Kids were screaming now. But the Jocelyns didn't mind. Like it wasn't even any trouble they turned the kids they'd grabbed upside down and held them by the ankles and shook them like they were trying to shake money out of a couple of piggy banks.

"Stop it!" we all yelled.

"Don't worry, be HAPPY," the Jocelyns sang. Pocket money rained down from the kids. The Jocelyns dropped the kids and grabbed the money and jammed it straight into the biggest vending machine.

Too late, as the two kids on the floor scrambled up and ran, too late, as the Jocelyns jabbed the buttons, too late we understood what was happening.

Thunk thunk.

Thunk thunk.

Four more Jocelyns.

We didn't wait around to see these ones crawl out of the slot and hit the ground and shoot up to full size. We got out of there. We scooted, we skedaddled, we scrammed, we split. We vamoosed, we high-tailed it, we made like trees and leaved. We ran.

Our mistake, see, was that we had just sort of assumed that the monster vending machine had swallowed Jocelyn for good.

Well, it *was* a lot bigger than she was.

But Jocelyn was—

We didn't want to think it.

When we couldn't run anymore we leaned against trees and looked at each other. And we all looked shiny fishy greenish white, our faces like a bunch of egg-shaped liquid crystal displays. Sick.

Nobody knew what to say.

"I bet the machine put up a good fight," somebody said finally.

"Yeah," somebody else agreed.

There must have been one monster whopper of a fight inside that steel belly before the machine found out it was no match for Jocelyn.

Before it found out that Jocelyn was stronger.

Before Jocelyn took over.

"Don't worry," a voice floated across campus from somewhere and from everywhere. "Be HAPPEEEEE."

So far the adults, the teachers and stuff, still haven't caught on that there's more than one Jocelyn. Even before Jocelyn came back from the vending machine it always did seem like she was everywhere at once. So even if a teacher sees one of her throwing tacos in the cafeteria and a few minutes later sees another one of her putting lipstick on the guinea pigs in the science room, the teacher just figures that's Jocelyn.

Her parents haven't caught on yet, either, because Jocelyn's smart. One of her shows up for meals and bedtime—probably they all take turns—and the other Jocelyns grab food out of Kwik-Marts and stay out all night and generally do whatever they like.

Vend U.

And what they like to do the most is torture us.

They pour tapioca pudding into our bookbags. Several times as much as they used to, because there are several more Jocelyns than there used to be. They steal lunches. Lots of lunches because there are lots of Jocelyns. We never have figured out exactly how many Jocelyns there are. Somebody brave went back to look and there are none left in that big machines at Vend U. So we figure between six and nine.

They make paper airplanes and load them with Comet cleanser and fly them. They yell "Mobile odor zone!" and spray us with Lysol. They climb into bathroom stalls and take Polaroids, then show them to people. They grab embarrassing underwear out of gym lockers and send it up the flagpole. They hold kids down and paint their teeth with green nail polish.

"Don't worry, be *happy*," they sing. And the funny thing is, they really do look happy. Not like before.

Not like when it was just one Jocelyn and all of us.

What's really scary is, now that they have each other, we hate them and they don't even care.

So they put salt in our drinks. Worms in our pockets. Nair in our hair.

One boy got so desperate because the Jocelyns kept putting signs on his back, I SLEEP WITH A STUFFED ARMADILLO NAMED SNOOGIE, that he actually crawled into a vending machine, the one with nail clippers Swiss Army spy cameras poker baseball fishing hats Parcheesi sets harmonicas rubber stamp printing presses folding bikes trips to Disney World. He crawled in there to get away from them.

He was never heard from again.

ABOUT THE AUTHORS

NINA KIRIKI HOFFMAN's short fiction has appeared in many magazines and anthologies, including *Bruce Coville's Book of Aliens* and *Book of Magic.* Her novel *The Thread that Binds the Bones* won a Bram Stoker award for first novel. Her second novel is *The Silent Strength of Stones.* She lives with many cats and has a witchball in her backyard.

JANE YOLEN has published more than a hundred and fifty books. Her work ranges from the slap-happy adventures of Commander Toad to such dark and serious novels as *The Devil's Arithmetic* to the space fantasy of her much-beloved "Pit Dragon Trilogy." She lives in a huge old farmhouse in western Massachusetts with her husband, computer scientist David Stemple.

LAWRENCE WATT-EVANS is the author of some two dozen novels of science fiction, fantasy, and horror, and almost a hundred short stories in the fields of fantasy, science fiction, and horror—some of which have appeared in this series. He lives in Maryland with his wife, two kids, two cats, a hamster, and a parakeet named Robin.

LAWRENCE SCHIMEL has written short stories and poems for over sixty anthologies, including *Phantoms of the Night, Weird Tales from Shakespeare,* and *Orphans of the Night.* He grew up on a horse farm with all sorts of animals—llamas, ferrets, goats, quail (and of course horses!)—and now lives in Manhattan, in an apartment which—alas—doesn't allow pets.

AL SARRANTONIO's short stories have appeared in magazines such as *Twilight Zone* and *Isaac Asimov's Science Fiction Magazine,* as well as anthologies such as *The Year's Best Horror Stories.* His stories and novels span the science fiction, fantasy, mystery, horror, and Western genres. He lives in New York's historic Hudson Valley with his family.

MICHAEL MARKIEWICZ has written several "Arthur and Cai" stories for Bruce Coville's anthologies. "The Wizard of Chaos" is his fourth tale about the adventures of the young king and his foster brother. Michael lives and writes in rural Pennsylvania with his wife, Lois Rebekah, and their two beagles.

PATRICK BONE is a retired parole officer who has worked as a ranch hand, minister, deputy sheriff, Telluride deputy marshal, prison captain, and college teacher. He is now a professional storyteller who writes poetry, songs, and fiction for children and adults. He is the author of a picture book/audio, *There's a Dead Boy in the Attic and Other Strange Stories.* He currently resides in the Smoky Mountains of Tennessee, in an old house adjacent to a small cemetery.

MACK REYNOLDS (1917–1983) wrote close to forty science fiction novels, nonfiction books, and magazine serials, including *Black Man's Burden, Computer War*, and the short story collection *The Best of Mack Reynolds.*

MARY DOWNING HAHN wrote the first version of "Trouble Afoot" when she was in high school and just beginning to think of becoming a writer. To her disappointment, her English teacher gave it a B minus, although one of her friends unofficially changed the grade to an A plus. Now, years later, Mary is the author of more than a dozen novels, including the extremely popular ghost story *Wait Till Helen Comes*, which won eleven state children's choice awards. She lives in Columbia, Maryland, with her husband. She has two daughters.

NANCY SPRINGER is the author of twenty-nine books for adults, children, and young adults, including the 1995 Edgar Award winner in the Young Adult category, *Toughing It*. Her most recent novel for young adults is *Looking for Jamie Bridger*. Her fantasy novel *Larque on the Wing* was the 1995 co-winner of the James Tiptree, Jr., Award. A resident of Dallastown, Pennsylvania, she enjoys writing poetry as well as fantasy and realistic fiction. When not writing she can often be found horseback riding.

JOHN PIERARD, illustrator, lives with his dogs in a dark house at the northernmost tip of Manhattan. *Bruce Coville's Book of Monsters II* is the seventh anthology he has illustrated in this series. His pictures can also be found in three of the books in the *My Teacher Is an Alien* quartet, in the popular *My Babysitter Is a Vampire* series, in the *Time Machine* books, and in *Isaac Asimov's Science Fiction Magazine*.

BRUCE COVILLE was born and raised in a rural area of central New York, where he spent his youth dodging cows and chores, and reading things like *Famous Monsters of Filmland*. He first fell under the spell of writing when he was in sixth grade and his teacher gave the class an extended period of time to work on a short story.

Sixteen years later—after stints as a toymaker, a gravedigger, and an elementary school teacher—he published *The Foolish Giant*, a picture book illustrated by his wife and frequent collaborator, Katherine Coville. Since then Bruce has published more than fifty books for young readers. Many of them, such as *The Monster's Ring*, *Some of My Best Friends Are Monsters*, and *Goblins in the Castle*, are filled with monstery creatures.

These days Bruce and Katherine live in an old brick house in Syracuse, along with their youngest child, Adam; their cats Spike, Thunder, and Ozma; and Thor the Mighty Wonder Pup.

ALIENS, GHOSTS, AND MONSTERS!

The scariest creatures you'd ever want to meet in six terrifying collections from Bruce Coville that will make you shake, shiver...and scream!

- [ ] **BAV46162-1** **Bruce Coville's Book of Aliens:** **Tales to Warp Your Mind**......................$3.99
- [ ] **BAV46160-5** **Bruce Coville's Book of Ghosts:** **Tales to Haunt You**................................$3.99
- [ ] **BAV25931-8** **Bruce Coville's Book of Magic:** **Tales to Cast a Spell on You**.................$3.99
- [ ] **BAV46159-1** **Bruce Coville's Book of Monsters:** **Tales to Give You the Creeps**................$3.99
- [ ] **BAV46161-3** **Bruce Coville's Book of Nightmares:** **Tales to Make You Scream**....................$3.99
- [ ] **BAV25930-X** **Bruce Coville's Book of Spine Tinglers:** **Tales to Make You Shiver**.....................$3.99

A GLC BOOK

Available wherever you buy books, or use this order form.